# SECOND SIGHT

DEBBIE MUMFORD

WDM
Publishing

# COPYRIGHT

## PRAISE FOR DEBBIE MUMFORD

**Praise for *Second Sight***

Inez from Affaire de Couer: Four stars; "This was an absorbing paranormal tale filled with suspense and passion. The characters were strong and well developed ... Paranormal and erotica readers alike will not be able to put this one down."

**Praise for *Sorcha's Heart***

Katie from Goodreads: Five stars; 'This story was fantastic...I strongly recommend anyone who likes paranormal dragon stories read this. Best prequel ever. Off to look for more by this author."

Old Ozark Gal from Amazon: Five stars; "...for those who enjoy a sizzling relationship without the graphic descriptions of what body part goes where, this is an excellent book. So what are you waiting for? Go read it!"

Karyn-Anne from Amazon: Five stars; "The romantic scenes were full of passion and heat, but not graphic or explicit. I really, really enjoyed this novella ... Very highly recommended!"

*For Bill*
*Thank you for your encouragement and unfailing love.*
*You believed I could write this story, and I rose to the occasion.*

Death has a unique stench, unpleasant and distinctive. The moment the elevator doors slid open, a whiff of the sickly-sweet, slightly rusty tang alerted Zach Douglass he'd arrived at the correct floor of the posh downtown Portland hotel. He strode down the thickly carpeted hall, followed closely by his partner. They rounded the corner into the hotel's east wing and the heavier reek of feces assaulted his nostrils. He grimaced, erected a mental barrier against the offensive odor and paced off the final steps to the open door of the room.

The uniform stationed in the hall stood with legs braced and thumbs hooked under his gun belt. His stance bespoke authority, but the green cast to his skin and beads of perspiration on his upper lip screamed unease. He glanced warily at Zach, dilated pupils darkening his eyes. Zach tightened his mental shield, nodded to the man, flashed his security clearance and slipped under the bright yellow crime scene tape.

The spacious room hid its secrets behind a swarm of investigators performing their meticulous duties. A quiet buzz of voices whispered into individual recording devices, providing a white-noise barrier to the outside world. Zach elbowed his way in, clearing a path for his petite partner. Moving with hive-like choreography, the crowd shifted to reveal a man's naked body in all its grim degradation.

The victim had been handsome, a young Viking with the firm flesh of vigorous health. He lay spread-eagled on the floor, his face frozen in panicked disbelief. A thin line of some granular substance encircled the body and crossed the victim's flesh at wrists, neck and ankles. The wound — a raw, gaping tear slitting the man's torso from collarbone to pelvic ridge — seized Zach's gaze. Body parts that should never have seen the light of day littered the plush carpeting.

Stomach acid surged into Zach's throat and threatened to erupt. He wrenched his gaze from the blood-bright scene, turned and all but bowled his partner, Angie Sutcliffe, over. Grabbing her arm, he pushed her out into the hall, sank to the floor and dropped his head between his knees. After a moment's focused breathing, he said, "Sorry, Angie, but I've never seen anything like that."

"I still haven't," she said. Her voice held a grim edge. "Tell me what you saw. It'll prepare me and steady you — help put things in perspective."

He nodded, took several deep breaths and described the eviscerated corpse. His voice calmed as he spoke, proving her right, as usual. A giant intellect housed itself in Angie's trim body. Five-foot-two — if she stretched — boyish figure, slim hips and small breasts. Short, curly blonde hair tumbled around a pixie face and framed the brightest blue eyes Zach had ever lost himself in.

Mischief often danced in Angie's eyes, accompanied by an infectious delight in life, but her unsophisticated appearance disguised a razor-sharp mind and an unparalleled psychic talent. Whenever the Institute for Paranormal Research needed a crack investigator on site, they sent Angie. Zach understood his role. He kept the skeptics at bay so Angie could accomplish her task. They made a good team, professionally and personally.

"Right," he said. "I'm better now. I can see a pattern emerging. The dead guy's been laid out in a pentacle. The salt — or whatever that stuff is — it's a warding circle." He looked up into Angie's blue eyes, which had darkened with concern. "Some serious shit happened in there — more than just murder, maybe ritual sacrifice."

She nodded and said, "Okay. I'm forewarned. I can handle it. If you're all right, let's get back in there and see what the room has to tell me."

Zach stood and his six-foot-two frame towered above her. "I'm fine," he said. "I won't lose it again." He pushed his way back into the room and broke a trail through investigators straight to the corpse. The color drained from Angie's delicate features, but her eyes narrowed and hardened with determination. She knelt to study the scene.

"I take it you two are the paranormal investigators?"

The gruff voice sounded at Zach's shoulder. The emphasis on the last two words held an all too familiar derision. Zach turned to face the speaker, instinctively side-stepping to place himself between the tall, rumpled man and Angie, who knelt beside the body, already deeply immersed in observation.

"I'm Zach Douglass," he said and offered his hand to the detective. "My partner, Angie Sutcliffe, is already working. I'd appreciate it if you waited to speak to her. Perhaps we could move over there, give her a little space?"

The gray-haired detective eyed Angie skeptically, but allowed Zach to maneuver him across the room.

"I'm sorry," Zach said. "I didn't catch your name."

"Lieutenant Anderson. I'm in charge of this investigation. Mind telling me how you two got here so fast?"

"Of course not, Lieutenant. I see you have our authorization." He gestured to the piece of paper clutched in Anderson's large hand. "We're from the Institute for Paranormal Research."

"Yeah, but according to this, your institute is in Seattle." Anderson waved the form in Zach's face. "How did you get here before the coroner even arranged transport for the stiff? Who tipped you off?"

Zach smiled, a tight-lipped little grimace. "Like I said, it's an institute for *paranormal* research. Certain of our members are attuned to crimes involving, shall we say, unusual circumstances. My employer sent Ms. Sutcliffe and myself down to Portland in his private helicopter when news of this occurrence crossed his desk. He arranged for our clearance while we were in flight. The final member of our team will arrive later in the day. She's driving down. We'll want our own transportation while we're here."

"So, you're telling me some freak in Seattle felt, what — a disturbance in the force — and your boss whisked you two down here on a whim?"

"I wouldn't call it a whim, Lieutenant." Zach bristled, but held his temper. He glanced meaningfully at the body. "You can see our information was accurate."

"Too accurate to my way of thinking," the older man said. "How do I know your informant wasn't involved?"

An inappropriate bubble of laughter rose in Zach's throat and he coughed to cover it, raising his fist to hide the attendant smile. "You're welcome to check her out, but our informant is an eighty-five-year-old great-grandmother. Mary Ellen hasn't left Seattle in, oh, I'd guess about twenty-five years, and I seriously doubt she has the physical strength to subdue a man in his prime." He coughed again and forced his face into a stern mask. "But by all means, Lieutenant Anderson, question her yourself."

"Don't think I won't."

"Speaking of questioning people, did anyone hear anything?" Zach nodded toward the gutted corpse. "He had to have screamed like a banshee."

"You'd think so, wouldn't you? But if anyone heard him, they're not talking. None of the people in the surrounding rooms reported so much as a loud snore last night." Anderson shrugged and turned his attention to Angie. "Here! What's she doing?"

The detective stepped forward, but Zach laid a restraining hand on his arm. "Relax, Lieutenant," he said. "Angie has investigated a number of murders. She won't contaminate your evidence." His gaze flickered to the corpse. Angie knelt just outside the glittering circle, eyes closed, face tranquil. Her outstretched hands skimmed millimeters from the victim's open-eyed face.

Anderson scowled fiercely and brushed Zach's hand away. "You didn't answer my question. What's she doing?"

"I can't be sure," he said, his hand dropping back to his side, "but I'd guess she's checking for lingering impressions."

Puzzlement settled on Anderson's lined face. Zach sighed and explained. "A really talented psychic can sometimes read a dead man's final thoughts, and Angie's the best I've ever known. She says it's kind of like a picture burned into the victim's brain. If she gets there quick enough, sometimes she can filter it out." A tingle crept across his spine and he shuddered. "It's nasty work, reading a dead man's mind. Most psychics won't touch it."

Anderson's shoulders hunched forward. "I'm not saying I believe this mumbo-jumbo," he said, "but I'm with the ones who wouldn't try. Sounds disgusting."

Zach shrugged. "I'm guessing the average Joe feels the same way about the medical examiner's job. But it's got to be done."

"Good point." The detective scratched his chin and glanced

thoughtfully at Angie. "So, you think she might be able to tell me who killed this guy?"

"I doubt she'll be able to give you a name," Zach said, "but if we're lucky, she might be able to give your sketch artist a detailed description. Heck, if the artist is at all sensitive, she might be able to transfer the face directly to his mind — let him draw it from memory, so to speak."

"No shit?" Skepticism mingled with amusement in the older man's voice. "If this crap is on the up-and-up, someone like her could be a real asset to the force." He narrowed his eyes and studied Zach's face. "Are you one of the head-jobs?"

Zach laughed, a quick bark of sound. "If you're asking if I'm psychic, the answer is yes, but only marginally. I have some psychic ability, though not as much or as well developed as Angie's or other psychics' at the Institute. I'm learning to open my talent, to maximize what I've got.

"*Head job*, though? Depends on your definition, now doesn't it? I'm a researcher with a degree in paranormal psychology. I work with psychics, but I study them while they study other stuff. I suppose that might qualify me for the title."

"No offense," said Anderson, flushing slightly. "I just wondered why you were standing here chewing the fat with me, if you were supposed to be examining the scene."

"None taken." Zach took perverse satisfaction in jabbing the detective with his next words. "Actually, you *are* my job. I'm preventing you from interrupting my psychic investigator's work."

Anderson stared at Zach with incredulity. The color drained from the detective's lined face, to be replaced by heightening degrees of angry red. Zach observed the play of emotions and judged his timing carefully. He spoke just before he thought Anderson would pop.

"Like I said, Lieutenant, relax. Angie knows what she's doing — and so do I."

———

Zach respected Angie's need for solitude during the short walk to the downtown hotel where their employer, James Towne, had arranged for lodgings. She'd been pale and distracted since she finished her initial reading of the young man's body. Zach longed to take her in his arms and erase the horror from her eyes, but knew better. Angie would turn to him when she was ready. Any comfort he offered in advance would not be appreciated.

They stopped at the front desk of the well-appointed lobby, signed in and picked up their key cards. Separate rooms. He and Angie might be an engaged couple in their personal life, but on the job, James insisted they maintain a professional demeanor. Zach doubted even a marriage certificate would change that particular nugget of company policy.

Sighing, he pocketed his card and escorted his silent fiancée to the elevator. "We're on the twelfth floor," he said. "Should have a great view of the river."

Small talk. He'd been reduced to small talk with his intended wife.

"What?" Angie's eyes cleared and she looked around the elevator in surprise. "Oh, right. This hotel has excellent views." She clamped her lips shut and stared at the floor indicator lights above the door.

"Sweetheart," he said, "remember what you told me? Talking about it helps put it in perspective."

She shook her head, refused to meet his eyes. "I can't share this. Not yet. I need confirmation before I say anything." She edged away from him, hunching in on herself.

Weird, this skittishness, like she thought he might try to wrest her conclusions directly from her mind. Right. Even when Kate joined them, Angie would still be the only member of their team with strong psychic ability. Her thoughts were inviolate and she knew it.

Of course she knew it. How could she not know it?

Zach shrugged and leaned against the opposite wall of the elevator car. The floors crawled by. His heart urged him to grab her and kiss the fear away, but his mind overruled his emotions. He'd worked with psychics long enough to know what comforted the everyday man or woman often threatened a person born with the sight. The Celts had named it *second sight* and recognized its dual nature — gift and curse. It all depended on circumstances, how the bearer had been treated, what the sight had caused them to see.

Today, Angie's sight leaned toward curse.

The indicator light blinked twelve. The car slowed to a stop and the door slid open. Angie bolted from the confined space and darted toward her assigned room. Zach pushed away from the wall and followed at a relaxed pace. He glanced at the directional signs, but knew Angie had located their destinations in her mind while still on the elevator. He rounded a corner in the hall in time to see Angie disappear into her room. He stopped in front of her closed door and frowned.

Well, fuck! She damned well better process quickly. He didn't intend to be shut out of her confidence very long. Grinding his teeth, he pulled his key card from his pocket and let himself into the room next to Angie's.

———

An hour later, Kate Blackman, the third member of their team, arrived with the car, checked in and wheedled her disgruntled teammates into going out for pizza.

Zach strode from the elevator into the large, high-ceilinged lobby and joined the two women he'd worked with on dozens of field cases. Instead of their usual camaraderie, an air of unease filled the atmosphere between his co-workers. Angie's golden brows pulled together above tormented blue eyes and she hugged herself tightly. She glanced up at Zach with a wan smile, but her gaze slid back to Kate before settling on the floor.

Kate stood a few feet away, chewing on her lower lip and darting puzzled glances at Angie. A tall, stately woman with flowing black hair, Kate embodied Angie's physical opposite.

A knot tightened in Zach's gut, but he ignored it. He clapped his hands and rubbed them together in a show of good cheer. "All right, ladies!" he said, forcing a bright, happy tone. "Who's up for pizza and beer?"

Kate cast a worried glance at Angie, but beamed at him. "I'm starved," she said. "Let's find food."

"Right," said Angie. She shot an unhappy glance at Kate, strode past the concierge and out the revolving glass doors, into the soft spring evening.

Kate's gaze followed Angie for a moment. "What's up with her?" she asked, turning her attention to Zach.

He grimaced and moved toward the door. "Long day. Particularly nasty crime scene." He pushed through the door, looked both directions, spotted Angie and turned to his right to follow the bobbing blonde head. "Stay off the topic. She's not ready to discuss it yet."

"Right," said Kate, moving into place beside him and matching his stride. Nearly of a height with Zach, keeping pace with him never troubled Kate. Not like Angie, who required two steps to each one of his.

"So she hasn't confided in you?"

"Not yet. This one seems to have her more off-balance than usual. Maybe food will even out her mood."

"I wonder," Kate said, so softly Zach almost missed it.

"What?"

"Nothing," she said. "I'm sure she'll feel better in the morning."

"God, I hope so."

Kate laughed, took his arm and the two of them dodged pedestrians to catch up with his unusually quick-footed pixie.

The restaurant they selected was compact, dimly lit and crowded, but the ambience vibrated with good cheer. The concierge had praised its reputation for excellent pizza and local micro-brews. Zach hoped the carbohydrate-laden comfort food would ease Angie's melancholy.

"By the way, Kate," he said in an attempt to divert Angie with conversation, "how did your trip to Ireland go?"

Kate's dark eyes turned dreamy and a slight flush colored her cheeks. "It was amazing," she said. "I met distant relatives on my mother's side, visited the village our branch of the family called home and discovered some fascinating family legends."

Angie stopped picking bits of green pepper off her slice of pizza and stared at Kate. "Legends?" she asked. "What kind of legends?"

The knot in Zach's stomach loosened and he took a healthy swig of beer.

"Oh, you know," Kate said with a wave of her perfectly mani-cured hand, "the usual superstitious nonsense. My too-many-times-to-count great-grandmother was a notorious witch. She made a pact with the devil and held the power of life and death over the entire village."

Kate's laugh refreshed the stale atmosphere and Zach's knot relaxed another notch. "What happened?" he asked, sliding his beer glass and plate toward the center of the table and folding his arms in front of him.

"Well, the story I heard said the village priest called in rein-forcements and they burned her at the stake." She leaned forward with a dramatic shiver. "But Gran had the last laugh," she continued in a stage whisper, "she wrote down all her secrets, secured them with her most powerful enchantment and entrusted them to her eldest daughter."

Angie sucked in an audible breath. "What happened to that document?"

Kate shrugged. "Who knows? I told you. It's a family legend. You know, the kind of thing to scare kids into behaving. 'Be good or Granny Mab will send her demon after you.'" Rich laughter accompanied these words and her dark eyes sparkled. "The document probably never existed in the first place."

Angie frowned, picked another pepper from her pizza and tossed her napkin on the table. "I'm sorry to be such a kill-joy," she said, "but it's been a long day and I'm exhausted. I'm heading back to hit the hay."

Zach pushed his chair back, but Angie stopped him with a hand on his shoulder. "I'm sorry, Zach," she said, "but I don't want company right now." Her eyes pleaded with him for under-standing. "Stay here. Take Kate out for a movie. Have a nice evening."

"Are you sure, sweetheart?" he asked. "Don't you want me to walk you back?"

She kissed his forehead and laughed, a wan, thin sound after Kate's hearty gaiety. "I'll be fine. I just need some rest." Glancing at Kate, Angie's expression flickered from puzzled to concerned. "Have fun, you two. I'll see you in the morning."

Zach watched her walk toward the door, stood and turned to Kate. "Excuse me a moment. I'll be right back."

He followed Angie out into the twilit street, caught up with her and pulled her to a stop. "Angie," he said in a calm voice. "You need to talk about what's bothering you, if not to me, then to Detective Anderson or James. Whatever it is, you can't keep it bottled up like this."

She avoided his eyes, glanced instead at passers-by, parked cars, the potted plants that lined the street with vivid color. "I can't, Zach," she whispered. "I'm not ready."

He grabbed her shoulders and shook gently. "This isn't reasonable, Angie. Whatever you saw, you have to tell someone."

"I know." At last, she raised her eyes and looked directly into his. "What I saw, well, it concerns me. I don't want to make unfounded accusations. I can't be responsible for staining innocent lives. I ... I just need a little time. I'm going to check something out before I go to bed. I'll sleep on it and tell you what I know in the morning."

Zach searched her face, saw nothing but honest confusion and concern, and pulled her into a bear hug. "I love you and I trust you. Go. Do what you need to do. We'll talk in the morning."

She relaxed into his embrace and whispered, "Thank you."

With a solemn kiss to the top of her sun-bright curls, he released her.

Angie smiled at him, squeezed his hand and continued to hold it as she stepped away. Their fingers barely touching, she turned with a worried expression. "One last thing," she said. "Shield your mind."

His pulse spiked and the knot in his stomach clenched. "What? Why?"

"For me. I can't explain, not yet, but I'll feel better if I know you're guarded. Just put your shields up."

The expression in her eyes made his gut ache. He sighed. He hated the initial fogginess shields induced, but his short-lived discomfort would be a small price to pay to ease Angie's anxiety.

Besides, once erected the blasted thing would stay in place until he dismantled it. He'd only have to endure the grogginess once. He pressed his hands against his temples and visualized stone walls rising behind his fingers. A dull ache pushed outward from the center of his skull, dissipated and left behind a hangover of muffled haze.

"Done," he said. "I'll see you in the morning."

She nodded, blew him a kiss and walked away.

## 2

_____

Zach woke with a start and patted the bed beside him. Cool and empty. Where was Angie? For that matter, where was he?

Memory rushed in to fill the early morning void. Ritual murder; Portland, Oregon; investigation. Angie had her own room, dammit.

This investigation stank of the occult and he longed for the comfort of Angie's warmth in his arms. He rose, showered, dressed quickly and called her room before he bothered to find his shoes. No answer. He glanced at the clock on the bedside table. Where could she be at 7:00 on a Sunday morning?

Puzzled, he dropped onto his bed and catalogued last night's events. Angie had left him with Kate at the pizza parlor after promising she'd tell him her conclusions this morning. He and Kate had taken a leisurely walk by the river, and he'd returned to his room, alone.

He ambled into the bathroom, combed his hair and thought about Angie's unusual reticence about the crime scene. Something didn't fit. He needed to find her and that in itself was unusual. Normally, he didn't worry about Angie. If he wanted to see her, he thought about her, and either she came to him or "insight" hit and he knew where to find her.

Frowning, he turned back to the bedroom. Something seemed to be blocking their connection this morning. The answer hit him and he slapped an open palm to his forehead.

Laughing at his own idiocy, he sank to the foot of the bed and pulled on his socks and shoes. He still had his guard up from last night. She'd asked him to shield and he hadn't released it. Shoes tied, he rose and walked to the window. He tore down the mental wall and focused his concentration on the petite blonde who had agreed to be his wife.

Angie. Vivacious delight juxtaposed against a dedicated desire to use her gift responsibly. Something in yesterday's blood-soaked room had extinguished her sparkle. No matter. She'd confide in him today and she'd bounce back quickly once they discussed and analyzed her findings.

Angie. His best friend. His lover. They'd known each other since childhood, been best friends their whole lives. A few long-time friends argued against the impending marriage, saying he didn't love her passionately, didn't understand the difference between loyal friendship and abiding devotion. Zach laughed and called them hopeless romantics. He and Angie cared deeply for each other, and their sex life ... well, the words 'fun' and 'adventurous' came to mind. What more could a man ask for?

Zach closed his eyes and visualized her pixie face. Gradually, the vision changed to show her mop of curls blowing in a sudden gust of wind, her shoulders hunched against the early morning chill while dew sparkled on emerald green grass. She sat on a park bench. A weathered statue of a small boy and his dog shone blue-green in the growing light. He'd seen that statue yesterday evening. Kate had remarked on it when they'd strolled past the park across from the hotel. He'd commented on the artist's skill in capturing the devotion between child and beast.

He grabbed his jacket and raced for the elevator. Angie needed him. He could feel her fear and impatience. He punched the down button repeatedly, willed the doors to open and forced himself not to bowl over the disembarking guests in his haste to board. At the end of the ride, he squeezed through the opening doors, darted across the nearly empty lobby and pushed out through the revolving door.

Not far now. He sprinted across the street and over to the park bench. The moment he reached her, he plucked her from the bench and hugged her tightly. She struggled against his embrace.

"Zach," she cried. "Put me down. There's no time!"

The instant her feet touched the ground she lunged for her scuffed leather backpack and rifled around inside. She pulled a wadded up, white towel from the bag and turned to face him, eyes shadowed and round with terror — a wildly disheveled pixie poised on the verge of flight.

"For God's sake, Zach! Get your shields up," she snapped. "Here. Take this. Don't let it out of your sight. Get it to Jenny Murdoch. She'll..." her words stopped with a gasp, replaced by a strangled gurgle.

Zach looked up from the towel she'd thrust into his hands. Angie's face turned a ghastly gray. Her horrified eyes widened and then dimmed. She struggled to pull air into her lungs. Her legs buckled and Zach grabbed her, supporting her all the way to the ground.

She died before they reached the dew-soaked grass.

"Angie," he cried. "Sweetheart? What's wrong?"

Realization hit him in the gut and he bellowed. "Angie!"

After a moment's hesitation, he started CPR, glancing wildly around the park between strokes and breaths. Deserted. Not a soul in sight. Finally, he gave up, pulled his dead lover into his arms and rocked convulsively.

Fingers stiff with shock and disbelief, he fumbled for the cell phone clipped to his belt and jabbed 9-1-1.

Angie refused to own one. What did a psychic need with a cell phone? He glanced at her face, but his gaze slid away. His mind refused to accept the blankness in her eyes. Never again would they sparkle with laughter.

---

Zach's heart thundered in his chest. His pulse roared so loudly, he barely heard Lieutenant Anderson's questions.

"What were you and Ms. Sutcliffe doing in the park?"

"Meeting for our morning walk," Zach said. Anderson probably knew he lied, but since Angie had been the only one who could answer that question, the lie would have to suffice.

"Tell me about her collapse."

"She handed me a wadded up towel," Zach began, but Anderson interrupted him.

"The one with the book in it."

"What? There's a book inside? No, I didn't know. I didn't pay any attention. I was kind of busy with Angie. Anyway, she handed me that towel and whatever was in it."

He stopped speaking. The words brought the event too clearly to mind.

"What happened next?" Anderson asked.

Zach drew a shuddering breath and forced himself to continue. "She stopped talking, gasped for breath ... She couldn't breathe. She looked at me and her eyes ... her eyes ..." He swallowed, leaned forward with his elbows on his knees and buried his face in his hands. "She was terrified," he finished.

Cold crept into his heart and settled in to stay. He shuddered again.

"She begged me to save her with those beautiful eyes ... and then, she ... she just collapsed. I caught her, eased her to the ground, did CPR, called 9-1-1. Too late. Nothing I did mattered. She died."

"Were there any witnesses?"

"What? No, the park was empty. No one witnessed her death."

"Well, I'm sorry for your loss, Mr. Douglass," Detective Anderson said, flipping his notebook closed. "If you've nothing else to add, you're free to go."

"No, there's nothing else." Zach rose and followed Anderson out of the room.

"You still going to be working that case?"

Zach's dazed mind took a moment to interpret the question, but when it did, his jaw tightened. "Yes."

"Good. Then I don't have to tell you not to leave town." The detective paused and added, "Just between us, we expect the coroner to rule your fiancée's death a result of natural causes. Once that happens, you'll be free to travel and we'll return her personal items to you."

He laid a hand on Zach's shoulder briefly, turned and strode away, leaving Zach standing at the precinct's front door. Anderson had fingerprinted him earlier — "just a formality, you understand" — and the coroner had taken Angie's body. There would be an autopsy. He'd be notified of the findings.

Zach pushed through the door and stumbled down the steps in a daze. He stood on the sidewalk outside police head-quarters: lost. He had no idea of the time or even the day. He stared at the street sign on the corner. The letters refused to form words.

Lost.

A car stopped in front of him and a familiar dark-haired woman emerged. "Zach?" she said.

He didn't respond.

Kate touched his sleeve. "Zach, come with me. I'll take you back to the hotel."

He stared at her. She seemed to be speaking to him, but her words couldn't penetrate the fog in his brain.

She took hold of his arm and guided him to the car. Careful of his head, she urged him into the back seat, closed the door and walked around to the driver's side. She slid onto the seat beside him, leaned forward and spoke to the driver.

Cab. That was the word. They sat in a cab.

Zach leaned back against the seat, not caring where Kate took him. His blonde pixie had left the world and her exit had torn a hole in his chest that refused to bleed.

# 3

A few days after Angie's death, Zach stood with his back to floor-to-ceiling windows that showcased a professional reception area. A young woman sat behind the desk. A single severe braid controlled her dark brown hair, while a similarly severe black business suit constrained feminine curves.

She glanced up at him, squinting against the glare from behind librarian-esque glasses. Sunlight overpowered the room on this cloudless spring day and Zach moved to provide her with a bit of shade. Relief sparkled in her dark eyes despite the flush creeping across her round cheeks and upturned nose.

"Excuse me, is this Dunbar Consulting?"

"Yes, it is. How may I help you?" Her eyes focused on his face and the color drained from her cheeks, but she locked a careful, professional smile in place.

"I'm looking for Jennifer Murdoch. We have an appointment."

*That face. Those eyes. The tiger roared approval, prowled his enclosure, tail swishing, and reminded her of his prophecy. He'd foretold this meeting long ago. She mustered all her strength and reinforced the prison bars that held him at bay. With an effort of will, she focused on the visitor's words, surfaced, and forced her brain to engage.*

---

"I'm sorry," she said, blushing to the roots of her dark brown hair. "I seem to have spring fever. You must be Zach Douglass."

Zach nodded, narrowed his eyes and studied her pretty face.

She held out her hand. "I'm Jenny Murdoch. What can I do for you?"

Nuances of recognition, fear and focused control flitted behind her eyes. Control won. Her expression settled into a studied mask and Zach wished for the millionth time for stronger psychic ability.

"I understand you're a genius with translation, Ms. Murdoch," he said. "Plus a friend recommended you. I have a book I need deciphered." He paused for a moment as the memory of Angie pushing a towel-wrapped bundle into his hands assailed him. He frowned, forced the vision aside and said, "I have no idea what language it's in."

Her blush receded and relief telegraphed itself through soft brown eyes tinged with gold. "I don't know about the genius part," she said, "but I'm a more than competent translator. Let me see the book."

He hesitated, glanced at the brilliant sunlight spilling through the expanse of windows, and frowned.

"I'm sorry," she said. "Is the book fragile? Susceptible to light?"

He expelled the breath he hadn't realized he'd been holding. "I really don't know, but I don't want to take chances." His voice tightened along with the knot in his gut. "This is vitally important."

She nodded and gestured toward a white-walled hallway. "Please, come with me."

They reached the end of the sterile corridor and she gestured him into a spacious room filled with warmth and comfort. A mahogany chair rail divided the walls into dark terra cotta below and buttery yellow above. Two large photographs of archaeological digs graced the far wall, studies in tan and brown. Forest green carpet cushioned their feet and silenced incipient echoes.

Zach moved to a large mahogany table and laid his leather briefcase on its polished surface. His knuckles whitened on the handle for a moment, but he mastered his emotion and withdrew the muslin-wrapped volume. With exaggerated care, he removed the protective covering and stepped aside.

Jenny pulled on spotless white gloves and stepped forward to examine the book. Her fingers caressed the binding while she ticked off details in a concise, professional manner. "Approximately eighteen inches square, bound in supple leather, no exterior lettering. The leather retains a nice elasticity, but my initial impression is of extreme age."

Gently, she lifted the cover and examined the flyleaf. "Interesting," she said. "In a modern book, this page would be blank, but this one is filled with runes, and they're positively garish. Hand-lettered. In what looks like blood."

She jerked her hand away from the book and rubbed gloved fingers on meticulously creased slacks.

"I've seen blood used for ink in other manuscripts," she said, glancing up at Zach, "but this is ... disturbing."

Color drained from her face, she gasped and stumbled back from the grisly pages. Without a word, she turned and raced from the room.

After a moment's hesitation, Zach swept the rune book back into his briefcase, stowed the briefcase on a chair seat pushed under the table, and trailed the panicked young woman in a ground-eating lope. She didn't stop until she reached the sidewalk outside, where she shuddered and gulped lungfuls of fresh spring air.

"Miss Murdoch?" Zach touched her shoulder lightly. Electricity zinged from his hand to his heart. "Jenny, are you okay?"

"I'm sorry," she gasped. "That was very unprofessional."

He took her elbow and guided her down the sidewalk. "Let's walk for a moment."

She started to object, but glanced back at the office door with shadowed eyes and shuddered. "Yes," she said, "some exercise will clear my mind. But ... I'll need to keep the office in sight."

"Of course."

They strolled down the street without speaking. Her breathing slowed and regulated. At the corner, they waited for the streetlight to signal their turn to cross. Once on the other side, they ambled slowly back in the direction they had come. When they drew even with the consulting office, they stopped.

Acutely aware of her elbow cradled in his hand, Zach waited in silence. Something about this controlled young woman awakened his protective instincts. It disturbed him that he had caused her discomfort, or rather, that Angie's mysterious book had done so. Either way, he was to blame for bringing her in contact with the blasted thing.

"I'm sorry, Mr. Douglass," she said. "I can't imagine what came over me."

"Please," he replied, "call me Zach."

She gave him a weak smile and continued toward the traffic light at the corner. "What can you tell me about your book?"

"Before I get into that, perhaps I should give you a little background information. I'm a parapsychologist and I'm in town on an investigation."

Jenny flinched, and his fingers tightened reflexively on her elbow. His profession held significance for her. How odd. Most people gave him a polite but puzzled smile when confronted with his title.

"Have you had other experiences with the unexplained?" he asked nonchalantly.

She glanced at the sidewalk, the upcoming streetlight, the little boy on roller skates. "It's not something I encounter in my work," she said, deftly avoiding his eyes.

"Perhaps," he said. They crossed the street again and headed back toward her office. "I think the book on your conference table will stretch the boundaries of your experience."

Jenny's face paled and she caught her lower lip between her teeth. They stopped in front of the office door. He hesitated to open it. Her eyes had gone round with fright again and she raised her head and sniffed, as if scenting a predatory animal.

---

*Blood-soaked pages exuded a tang of rusty iron — almost strong enough to taste, definitely strong enough to pollute the sweet floral scent of the spring day. She'd managed a deft half-truth in response to his question. The ease of the lie pleased and frightened her at the same time, just as the macabre book simultaneously drew and repelled her. This man with the eerily familiar face signaled the end of her hard-won peace of mind, yet the tiger purred, completely at ease. That worried her; perhaps more than the horrible book lurking in the conference room.*

## 4

Cocooned in awkwardness, Zach and Jenny hesitated on the sidewalk in front of the consulting office. The constrained atmosphere abraded Zach's nerves, but how to break the spell? A gruff male voice rescued him.

"Jenny? Jennifer Elaine."

They startled and glanced in the direction of an older gentleman with wispy white hair and the leathery skin of one who has spent too much time exposed to the elements.

"What are you doing loitering on the sidewalk?" he said. "We've got a business to run."

Color bloomed on Jenny's cheeks. The petal-pink stain touched the wound in Zach's heart. He probed the injury, anticipating a hammer strike of pain. Instead, something stirred within and whispered reassurances.

*Good. A friend. An ally,* said a tiny voice. *Shields up … always. She'll help.*

What the hell? The voice sounded eerily like Angie's. Zach's gut knotted, but he refused to acknowledge the uneasy feeling. Instead, he studied Jenny. This young woman, with her rigid control and blushing cheeks, awakened his protective instincts.

He scowled. He didn't know this woman. He had no reason to be concerned about her. Someone else should protect her if she needed protection. His brain had no business sending him messages about her — especially not in Angie's voice.

The older gentleman stopped beside them and studied Zach with unfriendly eyes. Jenny took the man's large, weather-roughened hand, kissed his ruddy cheek and made the introductions.

"Uncle Andrew, this is Zach Douglass, a potential client. Zach, my uncle, Dr. Andrew Dunbar."

Zach extended his hand and observed the word "client" work its magic on Dunbar's expression. Long years spent in archaeological digs had weathered every inch of exposed skin, and extended time squinting in bright sunlight had produced a wealth of fine wrinkles around his eyes, but the vigor of Dunbar's handshake belied his advanced age.

"A pleasure, sir," Zach said. "I'm familiar with your reputation from the scientific journals. It's not every day I get to shake the hand of a world-renowned archaeologist."

Dunbar's face colored slightly and his feathery white brows drew together in a small scowl. "Enough flattery, Mr. Douglass," he said. "Please, come inside and tell us how we can be of service." He opened the door, and the two men paused, waiting for Jenny to enter first.

She hesitated, clearly unwilling to re-enter the building. Taking a deep breath, she stepped inside.

---

*Nausea rolled over her in a punishing wave. She pressed her hands to her stomach and willed Uncle Andrew not to notice her distress. Malice and filth radiated from the conference room. She sank into one of the waiting room chairs, unable to remain standing under the debilitating onslaught.*

*Her tiger strengthened, feeding on the energy surging from the rune book. Jenny gathered all the discipline she'd garnered from years of meditation and pushed him back behind bars in a far corner of her mind. She refused to relinquish control. Not now. Not in front of this man whose face had haunted her dreams for so many years.*

---

Zach observed Jenny covertly. When Dunbar turned away, searching for a book on the shelves lining the wall opposite the entrance, he studied her openly, fascinated by her struggle to control ... something. Whatever hid behind her pretty face, dominating it cost her dearly.

Jenny lifted her chin and glared at Zach. Defiance seared his mind despite his best shields. She all but dared him to mention her distress. The power behind her sending startled him, but he gave a barely perceptible nod. Relief and gratitude sparkled in her eyes.

Dunbar turned and joined their circle once more.

"I think you'll find this account fascinating," he said to Zach. "These particular ruins were of a Scottish castle. When we dug to the sub-layers, we found a wealth of Celtic artifacts. Fascinating people, the Celts."

Zach pulled his gaze from Jenny and nodded to Dunbar. "Yes, they are. I did graduate work at the University of Edinburgh. The Scots are an amazing people."

"Did you, now? What did you study?"

"I completed a research fellowship in parapsychology," he said. "It's one of the few universities in the world that recognizes the scientific validity of paranormal research."

Dunbar fell silent, a closed expression on his face. After a moment he said, "I see. So, you're one of those ghost hunters?"

*Her heart hammered. She should have warned him, should have told him not to mention his profession. Now Uncle Andrew's opinion of the tall, somber man had taken a nosedive.*

*Jenny clamped her emotions back under control and wondered why she cared what her uncle thought of this stranger. His high-cheekboned face with its dark eyes, slightly crooked nose and cleft chin might be familiar from dreams, but she knew nothing of the man. Zach Douglass meant nothing to her.*

*The tiger broke his bonds and pounced, forcing Jenny to acknowl-edge the lie. She shoved the beast back into restraints, but gave grudging acknowledgement to his perception. She couldn't fool her tiger — she'd been anticipating Zach's arrival since he'd first visited her dreams at the troubled age of sixteen.*

## 5

Z ach Douglass parked his gunmetal gray Jeep across the
street from Dunbar Consulting Services and studied
the nondescript brick building. His mind whirled with
uncharacteristic indecision. He needed the rune book translated
and by all accounts Jenny Murdoch was the best in the North-
west at deciphering obscure documents. Some experts considered her the best in the nation. Besides, Angie had told him to
find Jenny and Angie's echo urged him to trust the woman.

Jenny had been badly upset yesterday and Zach had seen far
too many bizarre things in his five years of paranormal research
to discount her unease. Truth be told, her acute reaction frightened him, coming so close after Angie's death.

He laid a hand on the dark leather of his briefcase and
wondered why Angie and now her echo — or could it be her
ghost? — insisted he remain shielded in the presence of those
runes. What had this book revealed to her while he had slept
peacefully in his hotel room? Nothing good, he felt sure. Angie
had been desperate and frightened before her death, and this
rune book held the key.

Jenny Murdoch possessed a strong psychic gift. She'd

demonstrated that yesterday. His shields might not be the strongest, but she'd sent to him as if they didn't exist. And yet he'd walked into her office and taken her completely by surprise, which argued against paranormal ability. Most psychics had an annoying habit of watching the door expectantly and greeting visitors with a knowing smile. He also couldn't deny the strength of her reaction to that blasted book.

The woman puzzled him. He'd initially considered her a little odd, though self- possessed, but her panicked escape from the building had shattered the impression of level-headedness. She'd been terrified of that damned book.

But considering Jenny was psychic, her momentary hysteria might have been reasonable. That book had something to do with more than one death. Of this, Zach was certain.

He remembered the way the tinge of gold at the edges of Jenny's brown eyes had turned molten when she silently dared him to mention her unease to Dunbar. How could her uncle have missed her distress? Zach had a feeling Jenny Murdoch kept a lot about herself tightly restrained, but for what reason?

Zach gathered up his jacket and briefcase. He couldn't lounge around all day trying to figure this woman out. He had a murder to solve. Two, in fact. Angie deserved his finest effort.

Angie...

His gut turned to ice. His best friend, the woman he'd planned to marry, had been dead less than a week, and a whisper inside his mind mimicked her voice and urged him to trust Jenny Murdoch. When had Angie and Jenny met? And why did Angie's echo stimulate such strong protective feelings for the woman?

He embraced the ice clutching his core and turned it into a hard, impenetrable shell. He'd need its protection when he asked Jenny to take another look at the rune book.

Jenny glanced up when Zach strode through the door. His tall form filled the doorway and her world sparkled with possibility. At the same time, the book he carried called her tiger from bondage. The tiny hairs along the nape of her neck leapt to attention. She marshaled all her strength to push both terror and elation from her mind and rose to greet her client.

"Good morning, Zach," she said, managing a polite smile. "Shall we start your translation now?"

Zach studied her with a soul-piercing gaze. Her ego squirmed under his scrutiny, but her expression remained impassive — a practiced skill. Finally, he relented and shrugged his broad shoulders.

"It's up to you, Miss Murdoch. You had a bad reaction to the book yesterday." He held up his hand to ward off objection. "I'm a psychic and a trained observer. The book upset you. If you'd prefer, I'll take it elsewhere."

Jenny closed her eyes briefly, unable to bear the compassion written on his face. There had been little enough compassion in her life. Pity, yes, in abundance, but not compassion. She didn't know how to deal with it. The tiger paced in the back of her mind, awaiting his opportunity. Ignoring impatient growls, she opened her eyes.

"I discussed the situation with my uncle last night." She mirrored Zach's hand gesture to forestall interruption. "Don't worry. He gave me permission to decline the project. However, I believe I can translate your document and I'd like to try."

"Where do you want to work? Here, or in the conference room?"

"Let's go to the conference room. The enclosed space mini-mizes distractions." She nodded toward the wide front window and the pedestrians wending their way along the busy down-town street.

They moved quietly down the hall and into the conference room. When they reached the massive mahogany table, he repeated his actions of the previous day, withdrawing and unwrapping the volume with an economy of effort.

Jenny expected him to sit once the book had been exposed, but he didn't. She had the uncomfortable feeling he wanted to be ready for any unexpected action on her part. He exuded a strange mixture of empathy and reserve. His presence disturbed her balance and she had to work to banish him from her mind and concentrate on the leather-bound book.

Taking a moment to ground herself firmly in the here and now, Jenny drew on her white gloves, widened her stance and planted her navy pumps on the plush forest green carpeting. She gripped the back of the black leather client chair and basked in the room's familiar psychic aura. Her surroundings oozed comfort, and the man beside her, though potentially distracting, radiated warmth and compassion. She accepted his support and added it to her defenses. Armor fully in place, she reached for the book.

White clad fingers caressed the fine leather of the cover. She acknowledged the tiger's agitated pacing but kept her attention focused on the runes. She'd never seen this type before, not in any text she'd studied, or in any of the obscure fragments her uncle's friends had brought for scrutiny. She turned pages at random, stopping here and there to trace a rune with her index finger.

Her finger hadn't quite finished the journey across one particularly complex rune when she glanced up at Zach. She intended to tell him she couldn't help, couldn't find meaning in these symbols, but her finger completed the design and the tiger leapt free of his confined corner, bounded to the center of her mind and roared triumphantly.

———

Zach panned his gaze from the book toward Jenny. She shut her eyes, drew a deep breath, opened them again and reached for the book. He throttled his unease and concentrated on remaining calm. Understanding the importance of maintaining a neutral emotional field, he fought to suppress an instinctive urge to protect.

After a few moments of turning pages and tracing runes, she looked at him with clear, undisturbed eyes. She appeared calm, almost at ease. He breathed a sigh of relief.

Something feral and dangerous transformed her beautiful brown eyes. Its power knocked him back a step or two. A deep, growling voice issued from between soft, alluring lips and his blood ran cold.

"These secrets are not for the likes of you," she said. "You study, but have no understanding. You seek, but cannot use what you find. Beware, little man, you meddle with powers beyond your control. Do not be consumed by their fire."

The fiery light behind her eyes died and Jenny dropped like a rock.

Zach's heart skipped a beat, his gut clenched and air squeezed from his lungs in a tortured hiss. Not again! This couldn't happen again!

He dropped to the floor at Jenny's side and pulled her roughly into his arms. He refused to live through the nightmare again. He buried his face in her hair and memory crashed against his defenses.

Angie, giving him the thrice-damned rune book and collapsing, her beloved face contorted in terror, trying to pull air into her lungs. If his desire to unlock the book's mysteries had cost this young woman her life...

Zach cradled Jenny against his chest and rocked, his right hand curled around her wrist. The age-old motion comforted his distraught soul, and his body sought to fold in on itself while still protecting Jenny. There! Her pulse throbbed against his fingers. Strong and insistent, the rhythmic beat unlocked the agony in his heart and tears streamed across his cheeks.

# 6

J enny struggled to rise from the depths of insensibility. A moan escaped her lips. A sudden cessation of arguing voices pressed against her mind.

Her mind ... Was it still hers, or had she lost it again?

Waiting to open her eyes, she took a moment to survey her interior landscape. The tiger lounged in pride of place, firmly ensconced in the center of her consciousness. Her child-self, who she kept more tightly controlled than the tiger, squealed with delight and showered the powerful beast with love and welcome. Her rational-self, the rigorous comptroller of child, beast and emotions, cowered in a corner.

All her deepest fears had surfaced together, but how could she be afraid? The child giggled happily, the tiger lounged in content and the blissful warmth of Zach's concern bathed her while she snuggled in his arms.

Jenny's eyes flew open and she found Zach staring at her, his gorgeous, dark eyes full of concern. She closed her own quickly. Her pulse raced; the tiger stirred; the child whimpered. Jenny didn't understand concern. Uncle Andrew, who loved her dearly and would die to protect her, never looked at her with untainted concern. He remembered too much. His concern always held an expectation of mental instability on her part. Andrew Dunbar feared her tiger more than she did, impossible as that seemed.

She inhaled deeply, intending to quiet herself with meditative techniques, but the tiger roared. She exhaled a shuddering sob. Zach pulled her closer into his embrace.

"You're safe, Jenny," he whispered. "Come back to us."

The tiger stood, head lowered, hackles raised, and Jenny capitulated. She released control and allowed Zach's concern to wash over her troubled soul. The tiger circled once and gracefully lowered himself to a prone position, purring with loud satisfaction.

She opened her eyes and smiled at Zach Douglass, the man her tiger not only approved of, but had anxiously awaited.

"Jennifer Elaine! Oh God, Jenny? Are you alright?"

She tore her gaze from Zach's face and glanced at Uncle Andrew. She remembered the sudden quiet that had greeted her return to consciousness. They'd been talking when she awoke, perhaps arguing. Before she could say anything, another voice spoke, a female voice.

"Is she okay, Zach?"

The tiger's purring died. He raised his head and sniffed the air. Jenny recognized possessiveness in the woman's tone. The newcomer considered Zach her own. Jenny's presence in Zach's arms annoyed the other female, though the woman tried to disguise displeasure with concern.

Jenny frowned. Where had that insight come from?

The tiger's purr revved proudly and understanding blossomed. He could tell her many things. She only needed to listen.

"She's going to be fine, aren't you, Jenny?" Zach brushed her hair from her eyes, thereby reclaiming her attention.

"Yes," she said, smiling once more. "I'm fine." She struggled to rise, but only for propriety's sake. If Uncle Andrew and the unknown woman hadn't been in the room, Jenny could've stayed in Zach's arms indefinitely. She liked his warmth and the way he held her. She couldn't remember the last time she'd been embraced and rocked.

Zach shifted his weight and helped her sit, but placed a restraining hand on her shoulder. "Don't try to stand too soon," he said quietly. "We don't want you passing out again."

She nodded and pulled her legs in to sit tailor fashion on the plush carpeting. Zach stood, and her eyes followed him up. She forced her gaze from him and studied the unknown woman.

Tall and slim, the woman had even features and a peaches-and-cream complexion. Silky black hair cascaded to her waist and her eyes shone sapphire blue. A beautiful woman, but Jenny's tiger whuffled his distaste.

"Kate. I see you got my message." Zach's voice sounded cool, his words calm and professional. No attraction registered from him.

Jenny flushed. This unexpected information pleased but embarrassed her. The tiger snorted once and stretched languorously.

"Dr. Dunbar, Jenny, I'd like you to meet my associate, Kate Blackman. Kate, this is Dr. Andrew Dunbar and his niece, Jennifer Murdoch."

Uncle Andrew nodded to the woman. "Miss Blackman," he murmured politely, but the tiger alerted Jenny to Uncle Andrew's more than polite interest.

She shook her head and scowled inwardly at her tiger. He'd given her entirely too much information. The tiger dropped his head between his paws and closed his eyes. Jenny's perceptions snapped back to normal. She took a deep breath and scrambled to stand.

"Miss Blackman, I'm sorry for causing such a scene." She

smiled and extended her hand. "I hope you won't hold this against me."

"Not at all, Jenny," Kate said with a pleasant smile. "May I call you Jenny?" At Jenny's nod, she continued. "I'm just glad you're all right. And please, call me Kate."

"Fine," said Uncle Andrew. "Now that the introductions are finished, why don't you gather up your book and leave? It's obvious Jenny isn't going to be able to help you, and I won't have her upset."

Zach stiffened. "Now see here, Dunbar..."

"Uncle Andrew," Jenny interrupted, "you're mistaken. I can translate the volume. Whatever happened, it's over now."

She met each gaze momentarily, turned and, before anyone could protest, picked up the book.

"See? It's not hurting me, and I'm certainly not damaging it." She hugged the volume to her chest. "Now, why don't you all run along and let me have some quiet so I can get on with my work?"

## 7

Zach broke the stunned tableeau. "Fine," he said. "Kate, check in with the Seattle office. See if they've finished the research we requested on the police analysis of those crime scene samples. Meet me at our temporary office in about an hour. I have a few details I want to iron out with Dr. Dunbar."

Kate glanced at Jenny, who was already seated at the conference room computer with the book spread open between monitor and keyboard.

"Okay, I'll see you later," Kate said and marched from the room.

Zach turned to Andrew Dunbar. "May I speak to you privately, sir?"

Dunbar scowled, but led Zach to his office. Once inside, Dunbar closed the door. Paper littered the desk and artifacts crowded every horizontal surface.

"What do you want, Douglass?"

"You do realize your niece is psychic, don't you?"

Dunbar's face turned pasty white, then flared red. "My niece is none of your concern," he snapped.

Heat suffused Zach's face and neck. "I work with psychics everyday. I recognize talent when I see it." Rigid with anger, he took a moment and tried for a more reasonable tone. "I'm also a psychologist and I know she's putting herself at risk by denying her abilities."

"You don't know anything about her," Dunbar said. "If you did, you'd leave immediately and never mention any of this to her."

Zach pounced on this opening. "Why? What are you afraid of? Her talent is real. You should be helping her learn to deal with it."

Dunbar circled the desk and dropped into his chair. The high color drained from his face. Zach could almost see the thoughts racing across the older man's mind.

"You're not going to drop this, are you?" Dunbar said.

"No, sir, I'm not."

"Then sit down. Let me see if I can convince you of the need to do just that."

Zach cleared a stack of books from a worn leather chair and sat. He'd seen family members persecute psychics. He hoped Dunbar didn't fall into that category.

Dunbar expelled a long breath. "You have to understand. This all happened a long time ago and I was out of the country. Jenny witnessed everything, but she won't speak of it." His voice trailed off and his eyes softened.

"Jenny was twelve. She lived here in Portland with her father and mother — my sister. I was in Tibet doing field preparation for a major archaeological dig. By the time I received the news, everything had been set in motion. Even if I'd been here, I don't think I could've changed the outcome..."

Zach waited a moment and then asked quietly, "What happened, sir?"

Dunbar shrugged his shoulders and focused on Zach.

"Sorry. The memory is painful." His tongue darted rapidly around the perimeter of his mouth and disappeared behind the tight line of his lips.

"Take your time, sir."

"My sister and her husband died in a fire at a friend's penthouse. When the authorities went to their home, they found Jenny with a baby-sitter. The child evidently suffered a complete collapse when they broke the news to her. Kept insisting she'd killed them." Dunbar kneaded his forehead with his right hand. "By the time I arrived stateside, Deirdre and Kenneth had been buried, and Jenny had been committed to a mental institution."

The older man dropped his hand and glared at Zach. "I tried to get her out. Told them I'd be responsible for her, but even though I was her legal guardian, I couldn't stand up to the array of doctors. They said she was delusional and had suffered a complete psychotic break. They seemed convinced she'd harm herself if not kept under constant scrutiny."

"How long was she ... detained?" Zach asked.

"Four years. She was sixteen years old before I managed to get her out." Dunbar's blue eyes brightened with tears, but he blinked them back and forged ahead. "Actually, I don't think I had much to do with it. I think Jenny learned to play the game. She told them what they wanted to hear." He leaned forward, elbows on the desk. "I think she's still telling everyone what they want to hear."

Zach nodded. "That's why I need to confront her about her talent. She needs to face who and what she is."

"No!" Dunbar shot to his feet and Zach froze, suddenly glad to have the desk between them. "That's why you'll leave her alone. She's found a balance. She's happy. If she's lying to herself and to me, so be it. I can live with the lie. I won't have you upsetting her equilibrium."

"It's interesting, don't you think," Zach said in a calm, quiet voice. "You haven't scoffed at the idea of Jenny having psychic abilities." He cocked an eyebrow at Dunbar. "I expected you to tell me such nonsense doesn't exist."

Dunbar gave a little snort and dropped back into his chair. "It's a fuzzy science, I'll agree, but I've lived in too many diverse cultures, seen too many inexplicable things, to discount it altogether." He leaned back in his chair and steepled his fingers. "As to whether Jenny has the gift ... well, let's just say I'm aware of the myths about children born on Samhain. Traditionally, Halloween babies are blessed, or more likely cursed, with *second sight*. Jenny is a Samhain child and she spends a lot of time meditating to keep something under control." Dunbar shrugged. "I've never asked her about it. I don't want her worrying, thinking I believe she can't handle herself."

"I wish you'd trust me, Dr. Dunbar. I can help her. The Institute I work for can help her. We understand the tightrope she's walking."

Dunbar studied Zach's face. He shook his head, exhaled deeply and rose. "Whether you can or you can't is irrelevant. I keep forgetting. She's not a child anymore. It's not my place to make her choices for her." He held out his hand, and after Zach took it, laid his other hand on top of their joined ones. "But let me make myself clear. If she tells you to take a flying leap, I expect you to leave her be."

Zach met the glare in Dunbar's eyes with a gaze of equal intensity. "I'll push her, but I'll back down if she truly wants to be left alone."

"Fair enough." Dunbar gave Zach's hand a final squeeze and pulled away.

Jenny sat at her computer, the book of runes open in front of her, completely engrossed in scanning passages and running deft fingers across the keyboard to record her translations. Blissfully unaware of the heated discussion raging across the hall, she exulted in the harmony within her soul. Peace enveloped her, a soothing cocoon stretched from the roots of her dark brown hair to the tips of her stocking-clad toes.

For the first time since she'd become aware of him, Jenny and her tiger worked on a project in happy cooperation. His insight had provided the key to translating the runes, and their working truce had freed her from the need for constant vigilance. She relaxed into her work, at peace with her uncanny ability for the first time since her parents' death.

Her tiger slept at the moment. He had done his part. Now her keen intellect deciphered the code and drew meaning from the arcane figures. The mystery of the bloodstained parchment unraveled before her eyes.

She hummed to herself, a jaunty little Irish jig, until she realized another human had entered the room. Her tiger stirred, sniffed and settled again. No worries. Zach stood behind her.

"You're welcome to sit down, Zach," she said without looking up from the manuscript. "I'm making excellent progress."

Zach pulled a chair up beside her and folded his long body onto it. "I don't want to disturb you," he said, "but when you're ready for a break, there's something I need to discuss with you."

She looked up, startled by the serious tone in his melodic voice. She glanced back at the screen long enough to save her work and gave him her full attention. "What is it? I thought you'd be pleased with my progress."

"I am. Very." He stopped and looked down the hall toward the front door. "Why don't we take a walk?"

Confusion washed over her. She felt more alive, more vibrant than she had in years, but she still couldn't anticipate this man's moods. One minute he radiated assurance and the next he flooded her senses with indecision. Her tiger trusted him and she wanted to accept the beast's testimony, but dared she? The tiger had helped her unlock a translation, but could she depend on his assessment of people?

"Sure," she said. "There's a nice park a few blocks from here. We can walk over there."

She couldn't help but notice how assiduously he avoided touching her when he held the door for her to exit the building. The sun shone and the air smelled fresh after the morning's light rain. Late spring in Portland rioted with color and Jenny gloried in her newly acute senses.

They walked in silence for a block or so before she blurted, "So ... what did you want to talk about?"

"I wanted to ask how old you were when you discovered your talent." He spoke carefully, enunciating his words in a neutral tone.

"My talent?" Jenny hesitated. Her tiger stirred. She chose to misunderstand the question. "Oh, for languages, you mean. I think I was about fourteen when I discovered I could read just about anything."

Zach stopped walking and waited while she took a few steps, noticed his absence and came back to face him. "I think you know I meant your underlying talent, the reason you're so quick and accurate with your translations."

She stared at him for a moment, blushed, dropped her eyes and strode back toward the safety of her uncle's office. Zach's voice followed her.

"Don't run away, Jenny. I want to help. I swear, I won't hurt you."

She froze. The spring day curdled around her. They stood alone on a barren stretch of concrete. The air smelled stale, tainted by despair. The sun's glassy glare broke into shards against the sidewalk. The tiger growled and Jenny's delight in their cautious truce collapsed.

She turned to face Zach and the mask she'd worn for the last ten years locked into place. "I'm not running from anything. You don't have the ability to hurt me."

———

## 8

The murderer had been meticulous when she cleaned the room after the sacrifice. The only physical evidence the crime scene investigators had discovered — a single long dark hair — proved useless for identification. Though the follicle remained intact and the DNA exhibited the double X chromosome indicative of the female sex, most of the markers used for genetic fingerprinting had degraded beyond recognition. The dead man's partner had been a woman and the pair had been sexually active, but conclusive DNA evidence eluded investigators. The available trace evidence suggested the room had been scrubbed for the murderer's DNA — a physical impossibility. An act of God, or magic, would have been required.

Zach sat hunched at a black metal desk in his temporary office and poured over the test results the police had provided. A pattern emerged, one he didn't like. He studied and accepted paranormal activity, believed in things beyond the range of currently accepted science, but he drew the line at magic. It simply wasn't possible to remove all trace of one partner in a sexual encounter while leaving the other's physical evidence untouched. He definitely couldn't believe the killer had managed to disembowel a living man without a single person hearing the screams. The hotel had been practically full.

Zach looked up from the case file. Across the sparsely furnished room, Kate worked at a second cheap rental desk. She had linked her laptop to the Institute's data banks and searched for clues to a ritual similar to the one the murderer had performed. At last, she closed the laptop, stood, stretched and walked across the dingy office to peer over Zach's shoulder.

"Find anything?" she asked massaging her neck.

"Nothing but more questions," he said. "How about you?"

"Nada. Nothing like what you described has been recorded in our data banks." She ran her hands through her long, dark hair. "I thought the powdered moonstone would pinpoint it — most pentagrams are drawn in chalk — but no such luck. I didn't find any references relating pentacles to moonstone, powdered or otherwise."

Zach visualized the murder scene — a blood-soaked room with a circle traced on the floor in pulverized crystal. The victim's body formed the pentacle in the center. Heinous didn't begin to describe what had been done to the victim.

The gruesome scene still permeated his thoughts when the phone rang.

Kate answered. Zach listened to her end of the conversation and guessed their employer James Towne, founder and president of The Institute of Paranormal Research, occupied the other end of the line. She filled him in on the scant progress they'd made since Angie's unexpected demise.

Zach remembered his last encounter with his partner and his mood darkened. He and Angie had grown up together, had been best friends forever, drawn together by their common abilities. She'd always been the stronger talent. Her gifts had driven him nuts when they'd experimented and tested their limits.

He'd been a competitive kid and she'd bested him at everything they'd tried. Ultimately, their friendly rivalry had compelled him to study parapsychology. He'd needed to understand what made Angie tick ... what made him tick.

And now she was gone, stolen from him in the prime of her life, because no matter what the coroner's report said, Zach knew Angie had been murdered. He'd held her in his arms while she fought for life. He'd seen the terror in her eyes, but behind it, he'd seen knowledge. Angie had known her murderer, but the light in her eyes had extinguished before she could use her awesome talent to convey the information to him.

Zach breathed deeply, concentrating on filling and emptying his lungs several times. He pushed the memory of Angie's sightless eyes from his mind and pulled himself into the present. With his emotions under reasonable control, he gestured to Kate and waited for her to relinquish the phone.

Time to alert his boss to the discovery of a previously unregistered psychic, Angie's final gift to the Institute.

"I tell you, James, this girl's the real thing," he said after giving the Seattle man a quick run-down of his encounters with Jenny. "Even her uncle, who doesn't want to give me the time of day, admits she's gifted with *second sight*."

"All well and good, but don't lose your focus."

James' voice held an unaccustomed edge. Zach frowned, scrubbed his brow with tense fingers and wondered what had James so worked up. "Yeah, I understand."

"Your main concern is solving these murders. I don't believe Angie's death was unrelated to your investigation. Make sure we get the justice she deserves."

"Hey, this is me you're talking to," Zach said, his chest tightening. "I loved Angie. We were engaged. There's no way I'm dropping the ball on this."

James sighed and Zach relaxed a bit. "Sorry. I know how

close you two were. It's just ... well, I don't like losing one of our own."

"Right. Look, I promise, this won't get in the way of our investigation, but I'm not giving up on Jenny. Besides, Angie sent me to her. It's like she wanted us to meet, wanted me to help Jenny. You'll understand when you meet her."

"Do what you think best. Just get this one solved. I want you and Kate safely back in Seattle. The sooner, the better."

"Yeah, I understand. I'll call you tomorrow with an update."

Zach sighed and replaced the receiver in its cradle. The call reminded him of how badly the confrontation with Jenny had gone. She'd frozen him out. He'd been forced to return to this hole-in-the-wall office in defeat. He'd paced the worn, commercial-grade carpet trying to decide what his next move should be. The blank walls and nondescript rental furnishings hadn't lightened his mood. Finally, he'd settled in to study the police reports to take his mind off his failure.

James' call brought that failure back to the forefront of his thoughts, where it mixed with the anguish of Angie's death and curdled his stomach. He ached with Angie's loss, a dull pain medication couldn't touch. He should've packed up and returned to Seattle, should've told James to put another team on the case, but he hadn't because he needed to solve the mystery of Angie's death.

No one else would be as thorough, because no one else loved her the way he did. The coroner had ruled her death natural causes, had claimed she suffered a heart attack. Zach knew better. He knew the same maniac who'd mutilated the murder victim had killed Angie. What was more, she'd been killed because of the rune book. He didn't have evidence, couldn't put his reasons in words, but certainty resonated in his bones. What he didn't know was why she hadn't been able to protect herself.

He massaged his temple. Unanswerable questions made his

head ache. The fact remained; he hadn't thrown in the towel and returned to Seattle, and because he hadn't, because he'd followed Angie's final lead, he'd met Jenny and another set of tantalizing questions had emerged.

A slant of late afternoon sunlight from the office's single window distracted him. The workday had disappeared and he hadn't accomplished a damn thing. He tapped the stack of papers against the metal desk to straighten the edges and bound them with a jumbo paper clip. Too bad he couldn't clamp down on his preoccupation with Jenny Murdoch as easily.

She presented a fascinating puzzle: a psychic who refused her gifts, a girl who had endured unbelievable pain at the hands of the medical establishment, a woman who desperately needed his help to develop her gift. All true, but not the complete picture. Angie had sent him to her, but how had the women known each other?

*Trust,* the little Angie-voice inside his head insisted.

But how could he? Angie's demise had shredded him.

*Heal.*

Yeah, right. Was he supposed to heal Jenny, or the other way around? She was so wounded herself she couldn't even admit she was gifted.

*Help both,* the voice persisted. *Together. You ... Jenny ...*

He jerked the desk drawer open, threw the report inside and slammed it shut.

Angie's little echo didn't know squat. If she wanted to help, she'd tell him where she found the book.

Where had the echo been when he blew his attempt to discuss Jenny's talent? Why hadn't the ghost given him the right words, helped him put Jenny at ease?

Angie wouldn't have squandered the opportunity. His bright-eyed pixie would've known exactly what to say to gain the younger woman's trust.

"You look beat. Want me to get you some coffee? A coke? How about a shot of Scotch on the rocks?"

Kate's voice shocked him, like a splash of icy water to the face. He'd forgotten she existed.

He gave her a rueful smile. "Thanks, but no thanks. It's been a long day. I think I'll just grab those reports from Seattle, get a bite to eat and settle down in the hotel room to read." He picked up the documents, snagged his sport coat and strode to the door.

"Before you go," she said, "I couldn't help overhearing what you told James." She paused and Zach turned to meet her gaze. "Has it occurred to you that Jenny might be the murderer? The rogue psychic we're hunting? Doesn't it make sense, Angie sending you after her murderer?"

Electricity jolted through Zach's body. Jenny? A killer? He snorted his disbelief.

Kate stared at him, blue eyes glittering with compassion. "You said it yourself. She's been stifling her gift. She could be dissociative, prim little translator by day, sexual predator by night."

"Anything's possible," he admitted, "but I think it's highly unlikely Jenny's a killer."

"Really?" She cocked her head and gave him a sad little smile. "Is that the dispassionate investigator talking? Or the man who's captivated by the poor little misunderstood psychic?"

Zach's temper flared, but he held it in check. "You're out of line, Kate." He turned, yanked the door open and called over his shoulder. "I'll see you tomorrow."

# 9

J enny couldn't quite decide on a descriptor for her current emotions.

Elation? She'd found the key to translating the runes.

Unease? The emerging meaning disturbed her.

Nervous? Her tiger's continued freedom worried her.

Miserable. She'd lost Zach's comfort and concern. She expected to see him again when she completed her translation, but after the way she'd shut him down earlier, she doubted he'd seek her company again.

Too bad. He'd awakened all sorts of exciting emotions in her, not to mention precipitating her truce with the tiger. At any rate, these myriad feelings added up to one word. Too. Jenny was simply too keyed up to settle to her normal routine of soup and a good book at the dinner hour. Instead, she threw on a light jacket and walked briskly down the street in the direction of Mama Rosa's, her favorite source of comfort food.

A traditional Italian restaurant — complete with red and white checked tablecloths, candles in Chianti bottles and the tantalizing aroma of garlic and oregano — Mama Rosa's served the best pasta and pizza in the city. The restaurant bustled with dinner-hour activity, but Jenny managed to wangle a table for two. Carbohydrates and human activity. She found both in abundance at Mama Rosa's.

A ritual reading of the familiar menu calmed her tingling nerves and allowed her to center herself and relax. The front door opened and a waft of cool, flower-scented air mingled with the warm, heady spices permeating the room. She glanced toward the source of the fragrance and her gaze locked on Zach Douglass.

The blood drained from her face only to rush back with pounding ferocity. Zach chatted with Paulo, the maitre d', and motioned toward her. Paulo's eyes slid from Zach to Jenny and back again. Paulo nodded in agreement and Zach moved toward her.

In a flash of unexpected clarity, Jenny's understanding of the phrase "fight or flight" moved from academic to personal. Her defenses engaged. Her tiger crouched, scanning her surroundings for imminent danger. Simultaneously, her instinct to flee kicked in and her gaze flitted around the room assessing escape options, her choices narrowing with each of Zach's ground-eating strides.

Then it happened. Zach smiled and her fears melted in a blaze of joy. Oh, God, when he smiled ... The sparkle in his eyes spread across his face and pulled his lips into agreement. He transformed from ruggedly attractive to intoxicating. Her tiger not only relaxed, he rolled over, sprawled belly up and purred so loudly Jenny could barely think. Or maybe she mistook the source of the purr. Maybe her pulse sang in her ears. Whatever, Jenny knew exactly which descriptor fit this moment. Exhilaration.

"This is a pleasant surprise," Zach said when he reached her table. "May I join you? Or are you expecting someone?"

A small frown accompanied those last words and Jenny raced to remove it. She longed to see him smile again.

"No, I'm alone." She blushed, lowered her eyes and then boldly lifted them to meet his. "At least, I was." Her glance slid to the chair opposite and back to him. "Will you join me?"

Zach didn't waste a moment. He whisked the chair out and deposited his tall, lanky frame on it. "How's the food here?" he asked with a grin. "I'm starved."

As always, the meal defied description. Jenny relished her Spaghetti Alfredo and Zach made short work of the huge pile of spaghetti and meatballs the waitress placed in front of him. They laughed and chatted amiably, skillfully avoiding the topic of work, his or hers.

After the waitress cleared the table, they enjoyed a final cup of coffee. The relaxed mood encouraged Jenny to broach the sore topic, lancing it before it could fester.

"Zach, I'd like to apologize for the way I acted this afternoon."

"No need," he said, shooing her words with a flick of his hand. "My fault. I shouldn't have presumed to ... I mean I should have gotten to know you better before ...." His words trailed away and he stared into the dregs of his coffee cup.

"You couldn't have known," she said, "It's a very touchy subject."

She picked up her coffee cup and took a sip of the rich, dark liquid. The warm brew soothed her nerves and strengthened her determination.

"I can't remember what happened this morning," she confessed. "I remember paging through the book, deciding to tell you I couldn't read it ..." She frowned and blinked at him. "The next thing I knew, I woke up on the floor — in your arms."

A veiled expression flickered across his face. He replaced his cup in its saucer, rubbed his napkin across his lips and said,

"That's when I realized you're psychic." His eyes challenged her to interrupt. "Your voice changed and you said some things that, well, sounded like some sort of prophesy, and then you collapsed."

The muscle in his jaw twitched and the hand resting on the table clenched so tightly his knuckles whitened. Jenny didn't need her tiger's assistance to realize something about the incident had spooked Zach.

"I'm curious about what I said, of course." She reached across the table for his hand, but lost her nerve and picked up a saltshaker instead. "But I think there's something else, something you're not telling me."

Zach stared at her for a moment, nodded and said, "I'm asking you to trust me. I should trust you, too. There's a story behind how the rune book came into my possession." He glanced around the crowded restaurant. "But I'd rather not discuss it here. Would you be comfortable going back to your office with me?"

Without thinking, she said, "Why don't you come up to my apartment?" The implication of her words registered and her face flamed. "That didn't sound right. I mean, Uncle Andrew lives next door. If you come back to my apartment, he'll be available if we need to consult him."

That glorious smile transformed Zach's face. "Your apartment sounds great."

---

Zach tried not to think about the rune book as he stepped across the threshold into Jenny's third floor apartment and took in first impressions. Condo, actually, she'd explained on the way. Dr. Dunbar owned both his condominium and Jenny's. She had lived with him when they first returned to Portland. He had taken a teaching position at Portland State when Jenny enrolled for her freshman year. When she graduated with honors in linguistics, Dunbar had given her the neighboring condo, declaring that an independent young woman shouldn't have to live with her elderly uncle.

The living room reflected the controlled young woman Zach had met at the consulting firm. Very clean, almost obsessively neat. Subdued color scheme, calm blues and rose-browns. Tasteful, serviceable furniture. Nothing unusual or eccentric. He wondered if her tastes would change when she came to terms with her gift. He hoped so. He'd seen glimpses of energy during their dinner conversation. He longed to get to know the vibrant individual she kept so carefully under control.

He followed Jenny to the streamlined kitchen located behind the living room and savored the warmth of the small breakfast nook. Here, at last, he found a spark of the woman he'd discovered during dinner. The sunny yellow walls and white café curtains echoed the promised light of the east-facing window. The room would shine in the morning sunlight, and Zach had a sudden desire to share coffee with Jenny at the scrubbed oak table while dawn brightened the sky. He shook himself to clear the vision.

Jenny looked up from the coffee she measured into the filter. "Are you cold? I can adjust the heat."

"No, I'm fine. Just a wayward thought."

She tapped the measure against the can and replaced the cover with practiced efficiency. "Why don't you go sit down in the living room? I'm almost finished here."

A few minutes later, Zach lounged on Jenny's sofa, his long legs propped on the empty cushions while Jenny sat curled in an overstuffed armchair. Cups of coffee steamed on end tables near each of them.

"Now," said Jenny, "I believe you had a confession to make."

Zach grimaced at her word choice, but cleared his throat and said, "A little over a week ago, a man was murdered in a downtown hotel." He paused, watching Jenny's brow knit in a small frown. "I won't go into details, but it appeared to be a ritual sacrifice.

"The Institute I work for in Seattle sent a team of us down to investigate." He reached for his cup and considered his next words. "Angie Sutcliffe was assigned as lead investigator. I'm the liaison with the local authorities, and our aide, Kate Blackman, completed the team."

"Did you say Angie Sutcliffe?" Jenny asked.

"Yes," he said, relieved to have a reason to delay the inevitable. "Did you know her?"

"A pretty little blonde woman? Yes. We met at a conference last summer. She gave a talk on psychic phenomena and their relevance to archaeological artifacts. I introduced myself afterward and we had coffee together. She's a fascinating woman. Is she still in town? I'd love to see her again."

He took a sip of coffee and carefully replaced the cup, buying time. He despised himself for stalling.

"She died the morning after we investigated the scene."

He said it quietly, his gaze resting on the hand-knitted afghan thrown across the back of the sofa. He waited for the pain to strike, but the words merely reverberated against the shield Angie's echo insisted he maintain.

*No pain,* the tiny voice stated. *Relax. Help her ... help you.*

"Angie wasn't just my colleague. She was also my fiancée and best friend. We grew up together."

"Zach, I'm so sorry."

Jenny's simple acknowledgement pulled him back to the present. He glanced up, focused on her face. Tears shone in her eyes. A warm sense of peace stole through his body. Her compassion filled the void Angie's death had created.

"Angie gave me the rune book." He closed his eyes and revisited the scene. "She handed it to me, opened her mouth to tell me something ... and then her eyes went wide. She looked terrified, but she couldn't speak, couldn't breathe. She clutched her chest and collapsed. I caught her, but she died before I could get her to the ground."

His newfound tranquility fled. Beads of perspiration lined his upper lip and his breath came in fast, shallow gulps. His body tingled. He couldn't sit still. He swung his legs off the sofa, leaned forward and prepared to stand. The manic energy fled and he slumped against the cushions.

Jenny sprang from her chair and rushed to his side. Eyes clouded with concern, she clasped his hand. "Oh, Zach," she whispered. "How awful. I can't believe she's gone."

The warmth of her hand provided an anchor, a touchstone for reality. He struggled to find his way back to the peace he'd attained a few minutes before. Detachment, he needed to detach. He took a deep breath, exhaled slowly and found his equilibrium.

"You should know," he said, "she sent me to you. The last thing she said was to get the rune book to you. When you collapsed ..."

"You thought I'd died, too." She said the words easily, without undue emotion, but her eyes shone with understanding. She had the most beautiful dark eyes. "You thought the rune book had killed Angie — and that you'd let it kill me, too."

Zach nodded, bowed his head and rubbed his thumb against her soft knuckles. He hated admitting it, even to himself. When Jenny had collapsed, his first thought had been that he'd killed her by not warning her about the book's involvement in Angie's death.

She clenched his hand tightly. "I'm fine, Zach. Whatever

killed Angie, it wasn't the book." Her grip relaxed and she said, "Though it might have taught the killer how to do it."

Years of training kicked in and Zach's thoughts cooled. Calm rationality prevailed. "What do you mean?"

Jenny released his hand and leaned back against the arm of the sofa. "I mean the book is an instruction manual." Her voice sounded dispassionate, professional. "Most people would call it a spell book, magic. I think it's more of a workbook about using and strengthening psychic ability. Do you have any idea where it came from? How old it is?"

Zach shook his head. "No. Angie didn't have a chance to tell me anything about it. You and Dr. Dunbar would be better at estimating its age than I would."

Jenny nodded. "I think we should give it to Uncle Andrew after I finish my translation. He has the contacts to verify its age, possibly even the approximate region of its creation."

"Good idea." His thoughts circled Angie's death. "I know this is a leap, but I think the same person who killed the man in the hotel, killed Angie."

When she didn't answer immediately, he continued, "Of course, the authorities don't consider Angie's death a murder. The coroner ruled it natural causes."

"But you don't agree."

"No. I don't have any proof, but I'm convinced a psychic killed Angie. Probably to keep her from telling me where she found the book."

"Then I'm glad she died."

Zach froze. He stared at Jenny until a scarlet flush crept from her neck to her face.

"I'm sorry," she said. "I didn't mean it the way it sounded. What I mean is, well, if Angie had told you everything, you'd probably be dead, too." She lowered her head and picked a speck of lint from her trouser leg.

The moment of silence lengthened while Zach digested what she'd said. He'd been so focused on Angie's death, his own danger had never occurred to him. He might still be a target.

"I've put you and your uncle at risk," he said quietly. "That hadn't occurred to me. It's inadequate, I know, but I'm sorry."

"Oh, I don't think we're in danger," she said. "All we have is an interesting artifact. The danger lies in knowing where it came from and who had access to it. Obviously, Angie knew some of those things."

"I hope you're right."

She stood and picked up his cup and saucer. "Would you like a fresh cup?"

"No, thanks." He glanced at his watch and stood also. "It's getting late. I should go."

Uncomfortably aware of their proximity, he noticed the lavender fragrance clinging to her hair and imagined how the crown of her head would fit neatly under his chin if he took her in his arms. He squelched the image and frowned at the dishes in her hands.

As if reading his mind, she stepped back, giving him the space he needed to move around the coffee table to the door.

What was wrong with him? They'd been talking about Angie all evening. Angie, his best friend, the woman he'd intended to marry, Angie so recently dead. But Angie had sent him to Jenny and Angie's echo kept insisting he trust the translator. Still, he shouldn't find Jenny so attractive. Loyalty demanded he keep his distance.

Jenny walked him to the door, cup and saucer still in her hand. When he stood safely across the threshold, she said, "Be safe, Zach. I'll see you tomorrow," and closed the door.

---

## 10

Uncle Andrew sauntered into Jenny's office the next morning and leaned casually against her desk.

"How's the rune translation coming?"

"I've read the whole manuscript. I'm just writing up my report now." She stopped typing and lifted her gaze to meet his. "I've decided against supplying a literal translation at this point. The subject matter is too questionable."

His graying eyebrows rose. "In what way?"

"Well, its title will give you a clue. My best translation is 'gramarye'."

"I see. So you're translating a book of magical mishmash."

She smiled and returned to typing. "Something like that. At any rate, I'm not going to do a verbatim translation unless Zach insists on it."

"Speaking of Mr. Douglass, he's not bothering you, is he?"

She stopped typing again. "Bothering me? What do you mean?"

He flushed and fidgeted with a paper clip. Jenny stared at him in growing concern. "He said something to me about thinking you're psychic."

He dropped the paper clip and bent to pick it up. Jenny almost missed his next words "I told him about your history," he mumbled, "just so he'd leave you alone, you understand."

Jenny's insides froze. "You told him? About the hospital? About everything?"

Uncle Andrew dropped to his knees beside her secretarial chair. "I'm sorry, love. I realized I shouldn't have done it after the fact. Not without consulting you first. Not without your permission."

"When?" Her voice tightened. The control she'd relaxed over the last twenty-four hours automatically triggered. It didn't matter. She'd never see Zach again, not now that he knew her history, knew her to be a nut case.

"Why, yesterday morning. Right after your collapse." Uncle Andrew rested his forehead on the edge of her desk. "Can you forgive me, Jenny?"

Bright, golden sunlight illuminated her soul. She threw her arms around his kneeling form and cried, "Forgive you? Oh, Uncle Andrew! I could kiss you!"

Laughing aloud, she drew her astonished uncle to his feet and danced around her office with him. After she released him, he shook his head and returned to his own office.

Zach knew! That incredibly handsome, devastatingly attractive man knew the whole world considered her a few vowels short of an alphabet and he'd still joined her for dinner last night, still confided in her about his fiancée's death.

The thought of Angie brought Jenny firmly back to earth. Angie, his lifelong friend and intended wife, had collapsed and died in his arms. What a terrible loss. He wouldn't be ready for a new relationship, at least not right away.

Jenny walked to the reception area and stared unseeing at the busy city street. Zach's readiness wasn't the real question. The real question was whether or not she was ready for a relationship. She had never dated, never had a boyfriend. She had spent her teen years locked up in a loony bin, and when she finally earned her release, Uncle Andrew had swept her off to an archaeological dig. The only reason they had returned stateside was so Jenny could go to college. But even then, she had continued to live with Uncle Andrew. No drunken fraternity parties for her, no, sir. Fragile young women who came of age in mental institutions couldn't be trusted to the normal rigors of campus life.

And where had Uncle Andrew's over-protectiveness gotten her? Twenty-three years old and ill-prepared to deal with her first crush, that's where. Zach wouldn't be interested in her, even if he hadn't just suffered a devastating loss. He'd want someone bright and vivacious and bubbly. Someone like Angie Sutcliffe. Not a naive little linguist who couldn't handle her own talents.

Zachary Douglass might be a parapsychologist, but he was a psychologist first and she'd had plenty of experience with them. She'd be fine. She just had to keep reminding herself he was nothing but another doctor bent on examining an interesting case study.

Jenny sighed and returned to her office. At least she could interact with him on a professional basis. When it came to languages, she knew her worth. She wouldn't be at a disadvantage if she kept their interactions business-like.

---

Jenny had just finished the final formatting check on her report when a light rapping on her open door claimed her attention. She looked up to find Zach standing in the doorway. Kate stood behind him.

"If you two will go to the conference room, I'll be with you in just a moment." She gave them her best competent-linguist smile. "I'm printing the report right now."

Zach saluted crisply and moved down the hall. Kate studied her for a moment and then followed Zach. Jenny retrieved the report copies from the printer and stopped by Uncle Andrew's office on her way to the conference room.

"Uncle Andrew? Zach and Kate are here. Could you join us?"

When everyone was seated around the mahogany conference table, Jenny handed out the copies.

"As you can see," she said, "the rune book is an instruction manual for psychic techniques. Magic, in the vernacular."

"But this isn't a translation," Kate interrupted.

"No, it isn't. It's a report of my findings." Jenny returned her attention to Zach. "Given the nature of the information, I thought it best to be circumspect. If a literal translation fell into the wrong hands, people could die."

Zach's head shot up. "What do you mean?"

"This book details a ritual to draw psychic power from the auras of ordinary people. The folks involved wouldn't be harmed. They'd have no idea anything had happened."

"Then what's the problem?" Zach asked.

"That's for the augmentation of natural abilities. If the user isn't psychic to begin with ... well, there are explicit instructions for a ritual murder to jump-start the user's abilities."

Jenny paused to let this fact sink in. Zach gave a low whistle, while Uncle Andrew white-knuckled the arms of his chair. Kate remained coolly aloof.

"There's more," Jenny continued. "The would-be psychic needs to repeat the ritual every six months to maintain power. The good news is the ritual can only be conducted on specific days." She checked her notes. "This must be a Celtic manuscript, because Celtic-based languages are the only ones where I've run across the terms Beltane and Samhain." Remem-

bering Zach's Scottish training and Uncle Andrew's pronuncia-
tion drills, she took care to enunciate the Celtic Samhain as
"sow-in".

"Well, then. Someone's managed to decipher this before us,"
Zach said. "The murder we came to investigate took place at
dawn on Beltane." He looked at Dunbar and said, "That's May
Day, if you're not familiar with the term."

Uncle Andrew nodded. "I'm familiar with the Celtic holy
days. This means we can expect another murder at
Halloween."

Kate spoke for the first time. "Not if we find this pervert first,"
she said.

Jenny started, suddenly aware that Kate observed her closely.
She wondered if Zach had told Kate about her history. A question from him pulled Jenny's attention back to the matter at
hand.

"How many other people would be able to translate this,
Jenny?"

"I really can't answer that," she said. "It's possible that
whoever owns it belongs to a direct line of people who have
guarded the knowledge of this rune set."

"How did you break the code?" Kate asked.

Jenny flushed. She didn't know how to answer the question.
She'd had no clue what the runes meant until her tiger had
escaped. She'd awakened from the collapse with the key already
in her mind.

Zach answered for her. "Jenny is a natural psychic, Kate. I
think her gift helped her decipher the runes." He turned his
enthralling dark eyes on Jenny and asked, "I'm right, aren't I,
Miss Murdoch?"

Jenny searched for an escape. She wanted to flee the room,
fly through the ceiling, drop unconscious to the floor, anything
to avoid answering his question, but Zach's gaze held her. The

tiger stalked her mind, pacing, snarling, tail whipping from side to side. Still, she could not wrest free of Zach's gaze.

Gradually his expression changed, starting with those lustrous eyes. The light spread from there to his face and pulled the corners of his mouth into the radiant smile she had no power to resist. The tiger quieted. He remained alert, but his restless pacing ceased. Jenny quieted also.

Uncle Andrew and Kate seemed to sense the battle being waged. Each remained silent, motionless.

Zach spoke again. "Jenny, I understand your fear. The last time you spoke openly of these things, they locked you up."

*That's right,* her rational mind urged. *They tricked you with kind words then, too. Break his hold. Look away from his eyes. Don't trust this man!*

But her tiger sat quietly. Only the twitching tip of his tail betrayed his agitation.

"Trust me, Jenny," Zach said quietly. "I share your gift and I understand its burden. Let me help you learn to use it."

"You've already tamed my tiger," she said, speaking so quietly Andrew and Kate leaned forward to catch the words.

"Tiger? What tiger?" Zach stood without breaking eye contact and took a step toward her. "Tell me about him, Jenny."

"The tiger in my mind. He's so strong ... he's always scared me."

Jenny couldn't believe her ears. Could that be her voice? It sounded high and childish.

"Is he frightening you now?" Zach took another step and extended his hand.

Jenny shook her head. "No. He's out of his cage, but he's sitting very still." She cocked her head and smiled as Zach stepped closer. "He likes you. He's been easier to deal with since I met you."

"I'm glad, Jenny." He took her hand.

A searing blaze flashed through Jenny's mind. The tiger roared — not in anger, but in triumph — and Zach's face filled her consciousness. She experienced his presence with all her senses, through all the levels of her being. The tiger purred and she understood at last. Here was her destiny, the half of her soul her tiger had been waiting to obey. The realization hit with such intensity that, for the second time in too few days, Jenny collapsed into Zach's arms.

## 11

Zach eased Jenny to the floor. His heart battered his chest and waves of unwelcome emotion swamped his mind — elation, fear, uncertainty, he fought to think clearly. Mechanically, he reassured Dunbar and Kate that Jenny would be fine. Thankfully, Dunbar took charge.

"Kate," said Dunbar, "there's a pharmacy on the corner. Buy a packet of smelling salts and a six-pack of soda pop."

"Smelling salts? Do they still sell that stuff?"

"Just ask the pharmacist," he snapped. "He'll find what you need."

Kate ran from the room and Dunbar stationed himself in the doorway.

Zach fought to maintain consciousness. What had happened? His psychic ability wasn't active enough to penetrate another's mind through his own shields, yet he'd just witnessed the chaos inside Jenny's. He'd touched her hand and his world had expanded. There'd been a tiger roaring. He'd seen visions of himself in Jenny's arms, an ongoing succession of images. His senses reeled from the sights, sounds, smells and caresses he had experienced before she lost consciousness.

Too much to process. He desperately wanted to take her to a quiet place and hole up for a week, maybe even a month.

Why had this connection occurred now? He'd touched her last night. Nothing had happened. He didn't understand, but a thought flashed through his mind. He'd been foolish to think he could help her learn to control those sensations.

Zach clung to Jenny's unconscious body like a shipwreck victim clung to a lifesaver in a storm-tossed sea. When the paramedics arrived, they had to pry her out of his arms to examine her, and when they did, he slid beneath the waves.

He regained consciousness in an ambulance. Lashed to a stretcher on one side of a narrow aisle, he craned his neck searching for Jenny. She lay immobile on a matching stretcher on the opposite side. He tried to reach out to her, but restraints secured his arms. He continued his visual reconnaissance and found Dunbar sitting near Jenny's feet.

"Dr. Dunbar? What's happening?" His voice sounded thin and reedy, definitely not his usual strong baritone, but it caught Dunbar's attention.

"Just a precaution, Zach. Kate got nervous and called for an ambulance. They want to run some tests, figure out why you two lost consciousness."

A fierce light gleamed in Dunbar's eye and Zach knew the elderly archaeologist hadn't given the medics the whole story. Good call, that.

"I wish Kate hadn't done that," Zach said, his eyes drowsing shut. He forced them open and focused on Dunbar. "You'll stay with her? You'll keep Jenny safe until she regains consciousness?"

Dunbar reached across and patted Zach's booted foot. "Don't worry, my boy. They'll have to put me in a straight-jacket to separate me from my niece."

The next time Zach awoke, he lay in a hospital bed, covered

with crisp white sheets. The tang of antiseptic permeated the air and sunlight bounced off pale green paint some hospital administrator probably thought was soothing. The door stood partially open and he recognized the varied squeaks of rubber-soled shoes and metal trolley cartwheels in the hallway.

A movement beside his bed caught his attention. He turned to see Kate dozing in a chair. Her head was thrown back, turned with her cheek resting against the back of the overstuffed vinyl chair. He wondered how long he'd been out, if Kate had had time to fall asleep.

He studied his sleeping associate another moment and noted the midnight darkness of her hair. Interesting, both the women he currently worked with had dark hair. The similarity ended there. He'd never seen Jenny's dark chestnut hair unrestrained and jumbled, but he could imagine the effect. He turned away from Kate, closed his eyes and imagined Jenny, free from her rigid control, long hair streaming in the breeze.

"Zach, are you awake?"

"Jenny! Are you all right?" His eyes sprang open to find Kate standing over him, her hand resting lightly on his arm. For an instant, he thought a flash of annoyance crossed her face, but no, only warm concern glowed in her eyes. He chided himself silently and said, "Oh. Sorry, Kate. It's you."

"That's right, Zach. It's me," she said. "You're confused, but the doctor assures me there's nothing seriously wrong. You're stressed and overtaxed. You need rest."

She smiled, and Zach remembered why he was in a hospital. He wanted to wipe the smile off Kate's face. "Why did you call paramedics?" he asked. "Dunbar sent you for smelling salts. Why bring the authorities in when all we needed was a mild stimulant?"

"Are you sure you're awake, Zach?" she snapped. "What was I supposed to do? Ms. Murdoch was out cold — for no apparent reason — and you looked like you were losing consciousness, too. Smelling salts, my eye! Angie died with no warning and you expected me to go get a folk remedy?"

Zach glared at her another moment and then lowered his eyes. "I'm sorry, Kate. You're right. In your position, I might have done the same thing." He met her gaze again. "But in this case, you were wrong. A hospital is going to hurt Jenny more than the fainting spell did."

"Right," she said. "We'll just have to agree to disagree on that. I know I was right to seek medical attention and you're not going to convince me otherwise. Now, how are you feeling? Do you need anything?"

"Yes," he said, subduing his irritation. "I need to speak to someone in authority. I'm awake, alert and ready to get out of here. Can you find a nurse, or do I have to figure out these blasted buttons?"

He fumbled with the touch pad on the side of the bed. Kate sighed and pressed the call button. A few minutes later she retreated, leaving a fully functioning Zach Douglass to bully hospital personnel into negotiating his release.

---

Zach signed himself out and went searching the hospital for Jenny. Kate trailed along in his wake, but couldn't give him directions.

"Sorry, Zach," she said. "When you were admitted, Dr. Dunbar and I split up. He went with Jenny. I stayed with you. I have no idea where they took her."

His worst fears sprang to life when he found Dunbar sitting in the waiting area just outside a locked psychiatric ward.

"What happened?" he asked, seething with barely contained rage. "I thought you were going to stay with her, protect her."

Dunbar looked up, eyes bleak in the glare of the polished waiting room. "I tried, Zach. But she's an adult now. My assertions that I'm her guardian didn't do any good. They just looked at me and asked if there was a reason an adult woman needed a guardian." He buried his head in his hands again. "I didn't have an answer. At least, not one that would have helped the situation."

Zach dropped into the chair beside him. "Have you seen her? Do you know if she's awake yet? Why would they slap her in the psych ward?"

Dunbar rallied. "That's the strange thing. I overheard a doctor talking to a police officer in the emergency room." He leaned forward and touched Zach's knee, the look of concern becoming more anxious. "They said the two of you were involved in some occult ritual. The officer mentioned Jenny's long, dark hair and suggested the hospital get her into a secure area. What the hell is going on here?"

Zach froze, his face an impassive mask. Even his heart rate slowed as he fought to process the information. How had this gotten so far out of control? Why were the police involved?

Kate had called an ambulance. Paramedics should have responded, not the police. If the police had come to Dunbar's office, what items in the room might have suggested occult practices? What evidence linked Jenny to the murder? Surely they wouldn't put her in a locked ward just because she had long, dark hair.

The missing piece of information hit him and Zach exploded from the chair with a string of curses.

"That Godforsaken book," he cried. "They found that damn book and jumped to conclusions."

"What are you talking about, man?"

"I can't remember what I've told you," said Zach, running stiff fingers through his hair. "A man was murdered a week or so ago at Beltane. The scene had obvious signs of a ritual sacrifice. The police determined the perp was a woman. A woman with long, dark hair." He dropped back into the chair and massaged his scalp. "The combination of that damnable book and Jenny's hair has them thinking she's a murderer."

"Oh, God," whispered Dunbar, his face ashen.

"And you don't know that she isn't." Kate's quiet words echoed around the two bewildered men.

---

## 12

Andrew Dunbar stared at Kate in disbelief. "How can you say such a thing?"

"Dr. Dunbar, I admire your loyalty to your niece," Kate said, "but we have to look at the evidence dispassionately."

"What evidence?" Zach didn't exactly snarl at his associate, but his voice held a predatory edge.

Kate gave him a look that clearly labeled him an imbecile, and ticked off her points. "One, she's got long, dark hair.

"So do you," snapped Dunbar.

"Yes, I do. But I live in Seattle, not Portland, and Zach knows exactly when I arrived, since I left after he did and drove his car down." She gave Dunbar an exasperated glance and continued. "Two, she has a history of violent psychic outbursts."

"Now see here," said Dunbar, "what gives you the right to make that charge?"

"Forgive me, sir, but you were out of the country when her parents died. You don't know any more about it than we do. I'm just telling you what the authorities reported. Jenny herself claimed to have murdered her parents by psychic means. That's why they locked her up."

"They locked her up," said Zach in a low, controlled voice, "because they didn't believe her claims of psychic ability. They thought she was delusional. You can't have it both ways, Kate."

"I agree they were mistaken in their diagnosis, but their mistake doesn't negate her confession."

"For God's sake, she was twelve years old," Dunbar said, "and beside herself with grief."

"Where did you get your information, Kate?" Zach asked, his voice quiet and dangerous.

"I couldn't help overhearing when you told James," she said. "You do remember talking to James, don't you, Zach?"

"I do, but I don't remember telling him about Jenny's parents."

Kate shrugged. "I was curious and I haven't exactly been swamped with work. I spent an afternoon in the library researching Jenny's history. Amazing what you can uncover when you know how to do research. I'm very good at my job, Zach."

"Let's move on," Zach said. "What else do you think you know?"

"She's definitely psychic. She could easily be using the rune technique to augment her power."

Zach gave Kate a withering look. "Jenny's a natural psychic. She doesn't need to kill to gain power."

"Zach," she said quietly, "can you read the rune book? We only have Jenny's word for what it says."

"Jennifer would never falsify a translation," said Dunbar, through gritted teeth. "She has far too much integrity."

Kate ignored him and continued to stare at Zach. "My last comment involves you personally, Zach." She walked across the spotless linoleum floor to stand directly in front of him. "Think about your own actions." She placed a hand on his shoulder. "Angie has been dead for less than two weeks and you're so besotted with this woman you can't see straight. You're defending her, even though it's likely she killed Angie." She removed her hand and stepped back a pace or two. "You're not acting like the sane, rational man I know and respect." She gave him a look of pity and delivered her final blow. "She's been influencing your mind, playing with your emotions."

Kate walked to the waiting room door. "Think about it, Zach. You're too smart to be played like this." She pulled the door open and walked out.

Zach sat motionless, stunned. He knew to his core Kate had it all wrong, but he couldn't deny the thread of logic in her arguments. Jenny had experienced a disturbed childhood, and he *had* been acting strangely. She drew him like a magnet. When they were apart, his thoughts escaped back to her at every opportunity. He'd never experienced anything like this before. He'd adored Angie, intended to marry her, but she'd never consumed his thoughts the way Jenny did. Maybe Kate had a point. Maybe he was being used, manipulated by a psychopathic killer.

"Don't listen to her, Zach." Dunbar placed a hand on Zach's shoulder. "She's got it in for Jenny, and I'm guessing you're the reason."

Zach gaped at Dunbar. "What? What do you mean?"

"She's interested in you and jealous over the bond you're developing with Jenny."

"Kate is a co-worker," Zach scoffed. "Nothing more."

"To you, maybe, but I think she has designs on you." Dunbar stood and paced the room. "Let's look at her arguments rationally," the older man said. "There must be hundreds of women in this city with long, dark hair. Some of them may even be psychically gifted. Secondly, it's my understanding Jenny blamed herself for her parents' death because she didn't warn them of a vision she had. They weren't comfortable with her gift, didn't want to hear about her visions, so she didn't tell them she'd seen them caught in a fire. When they died, she couldn't be comforted.

"Three, we only have Jenny's word for what the rune book says, but you brought it to her. She didn't come to you and ask to translate it. You can have it independently verified and you'll find it says exactly what she says it does. As to you being too involved with her when you've just lost your fiancée ... well, I don't know you well enough to comment on that. But I've known men who discovered they were engaged, or even married, to the wrong woman."

Dunbar stopped pacing and turned to look at Zach. He studied him for a moment, and gave him a crooked smile. "That was quite a speech. I haven't lectured like that since I left the classroom."

Zach stood and approached the older man. "Thank you, sir. A little perspective is a good thing and, well, Jenny's lucky to have you in her corner."

Dunbar ducked his head, then peered up at Zach, his bushy brows screening his eyes. "My girl's had a rough life. I'd do just about anything to smooth the way for her."

Zach sighed. "I don't believe Jenny had anything to do with these murders, but I can't just dismiss Kate's opinion. What I need are facts." He nodded his head toward the door. "Let's find out if they'll let us see her. She's got to be terrified."

---

Jenny woke from a delicious dream, involving Zach holding her very close, to find herself tucked tightly into a strange bed. Shadows filled the room, almost coalescing in the corners, but they couldn't disguise her surroundings. She'd spent too many years in a sterile hospital environment not to recognize the stench of antiseptics.

Her worst nightmare lived. She'd broken her rule. She'd spoken of her tiger and now she had to pay.

Her world had ironclad rules. Loose talk of visions and uncanny knowledge landed you in the loony bin. She steeled herself to play the game. No one would rescue her. Uncle Andrew had tried last time. He hadn't succeeded. She had to fend for herself, just like always.

The weight of knowing what lay ahead ground her into the bed. Weeks, months, possibly years of twenty-four-hour performances. She grimaced at her tiger. He sat quietly, his lamp-like eyes shining in the darkness of her mind. Despair tore at her with each swift, jerky swish of his tail.

"I'm sorry," she whispered, "I enjoyed getting to know you." She had no choice. The tiger must return to his cage.

Why had she ever trusted Zach? If she'd resisted the temptation to believe him, to think he cared about her, she'd still be free. She knew better. Knew that where her tiger was concerned, trustworthy didn't exist.

She sat up, preparing to get out of bed and check out her prison, when the door opened and a nurse stepped inside. The snick of a lock preceded the arrival and Jenny sighed. Trapped. Locked in a nightmare. Again.

The nurse flipped on the light and glanced at Jenny. "Good evening, Miss Murdoch," she said. Her rubber soled shoes squeaked against the linoleum as she crossed to Jenny's bedside. "I'm glad to see you're awake. How are you feeling?"

Her voice, crisp and professional, held an overtone of pity. Jenny's chest tightened.

"I feel fine. Not even a headache," Jenny answered. "When can I see the doctor? I'd like to go home." She knew she asked for a dream, but tried anyway.

The nurse checked Jenny's vital signs, wrote her findings on a chart and said, "Dr. Adams is conferring with your family right now." She smiled and patted Jenny's hand. "I'm sure he'll be along when I tell him you're awake." She poured a cup of water from the pitcher on the bedside table, deposited a straw in the clear liquid and handed it to Jenny. "Drink up, Miss Murdoch. We want you well hydrated."

Jenny's fingers trembled against the plastic cup. Nice, safe plastic. Nothing to break, no shards of glass to threaten herself or anyone else. At least she wasn't being stuffed with pills. Yet.

The nurse smiled encouragingly and left the room. The door closed firmly behind her. Jenny held her breath, listening for the sound of the lock slipping into place. Silence pressed against her ears, and then the swift clunk sounded as the bolt slid home. Air hissed from between her lips in a sobbing gasp and she buried her head in her hands. Zach had betrayed her. She'd trusted him and he'd betrayed her.

She curled into a tight little ball and let the tears drain all thoughts from her tortured mind.

# 13

J enny sat on a bench built into the wall beneath the barred window. She avoided thinking about her condition, but the words 'abandoned' and 'hopeless' constantly broke through her defenses. The ubiquitous hospital gown and robe didn't help. They camouflaged her body in a blue and white bag.

She fingered the worn, coarse cotton robe and tried to distract herself with a game of "what if". What if she'd just been rescued from a week in the wilderness? Suppose she'd lost her pack and felt grateful just to be safe and clothed ...

The tiger stirred. He'd been remarkably subdued since she'd awakened in this horrid place, but now his orange eyes shone and his tail twitched with anticipation. Jenny pushed him toward a corner, but his strong aura fought her flagging spirits.

She wasn't a child anymore, he seemed to say. She could accept him and still be free of this horrible place. He would help.

He crouched, ready to spring into action. Growls and hisses issuing from his mighty throat left no question about his displeasure with her current lethargic state.

"Leave me alone," she moaned. "I can't save you. I can't even save myself. Don't you think I'd run from this place if I could?"

She buried her face in her hands and tears slid between her fingers. Sobs shook her slender body. She'd been betrayed. She'd trusted Zach and he'd betrayed her. God, how she'd wanted to believe he cared. She should have known better. She couldn't trust anyone where her tiger was concerned. Not even Uncle Andrew, though she knew him to be the one person who would never intentionally hurt her.

The tiger roared, and Jenny dried her face on the coarse cotton robe and pulled it tight around her body. Nothing could protect her from a sound wholly within her own head, but the action comforted her.

"You're wrong to trust Zach," she mumbled, leaning her hot face against the cool pane of glass. "I admitted your existence and he locked me up."

The tiger whuffled and relaxed his crouch into a regal recline, a king upon his throne.

"Fine," she said. "Hold onto your illusions. We'll spend the rest of our lives locked in a loony bin arguing over whether or not Zach sold us out."

With one swipe of a furry orange paw, the tiger retrieved a memory and held it out for her inspection. Uncle Andrew arguing with a doctor about the State's right to keep her. If only she'd been old enough to sign herself out of the institution, they'd have had to release her.

She sat bolt upright. "Wait a minute," she said aloud. "So *that's* what you've been trying to tell me!"

Jenny launched herself off the window seat and sprinted for the call button attached to the side rail of the hospital bed. She punched it vigorously several times, paused and repeated the sequence. Footsteps raced down the hall and she heard the metallic click of the lock being retracted.

"What is it, Miss Murdoch? Are you in pain?"

Jenny pushed her hair out of her face and smiled sweetly up at the woman's lined face. "I'm fine, thank you. In fact, I'm ready to leave. Please prepare my papers. I'm checking myself out."

The older woman's jaw dropped. She closed her mouth, opened it and closed it again. Finally, she managed to say, "I'm sorry, but that's not possible."

"Yes, it is. I'm an adult of sound mind endangering no one, including myself, and I'm ready to leave. The hospital has no authority to hold me against my wishes."

"But the police..." the woman began.

"I haven't been arrested. If the police wish to detain me, they'll need to charge me with something. Get my papers ready or I'll sue the hospital for wrongful commitment." She dropped the call button and moved toward the small closet. "I'm going to dress now. When I'm finished, I expect the door to be unlocked and my discharge papers ready to sign. Now, if you'll excuse me?"

Jenny had the satisfaction of watching a very confused nurse scurry from the room while her tiger purred and bathed his front paw with an enormous pink tongue.

---

Zach pushed into Detective Anderson's personal space and glared directly into his eyes. "You can't keep Miss Murdoch locked up just because she has long, dark hair."

"Hair color is only one factor here," the aging detective said, returning the glare. He held up a finger for each point he mentioned. "History of mental problems. Occult materials on site. Eye witness testimony to occult practices."

"What eye witness? You mean Kate? Look, I don't know what she said when she called for the ambulance, but whatever it was, she was mistaken. There were only four of us present, and Dunbar and I will both tell you, no occult practices occurred." Zach gritted his teeth, his fists balled, but he made a conscious effort to relax and wait for Anderson's response.

"Never mind what Ms. Blackman said. That's police business." He clenched his fists. A moment later he inhaled deeply, unclenched a fist and pointed a finger at the parapsychologist's chest. "I know you think you're part of this investigation, but you're not. We tolerate your presence." His expression icy, he added, "But don't get in our way."

Zach breathed deeply and buried his rage. "Detective Anderson, I'm not trying to tell you how to run your investigation, but the only piece of physical evidence you found was mine. If you remember, Angie gave me the rune book just before she collapsed. I thought it might relate to the case, so I took it to Miss Murdoch to have it translated. She's an internationally recognized expert, by the way. Once I had the translation, I intended to bring it to your attention."

"You withheld evidence?" Detective Anderson's icy expression solidified to stone. Zach refused to be intimidated.

"Hey, you released it to me with Angie's effects. You knew I had it."

Anderson turned to Dunbar. "Is this true?"

"I don't know about withholding evidence, but yes," Dunbar said. "Mr. Douglass brought the book to our office Monday morning. My niece spent the last several days working on the translation." He stopped, wet his lips with his tongue and pressed his advantage. "She forgets to eat when she's working. I'm sure her collapse was nothing more sinister than low blood sugar."

Detective Anderson pulled at his lower lip with his right hand. Zach and Dunbar waited in edgy silence and watched the police officer weigh his options.

At last, Dunbar broke the silence. "Detective, please. You can't know what Jenny will go through when she realizes she's back in a mental ward. She's worked so hard to put her institutionalization behind her. This is unreasonable cruelty!"

Zach looked away, unwilling to witness the naked emotion on the archaeologist's face. "Detective," he said, "this is just a misunderstanding. Don't allow Ms. Murdoch to be tormented over a book I gave her."

Anderson threw up his arms in resignation and then settled his fists on his hips. "You win. I'll arrange for her release. But make sure she doesn't leave town. I still have unanswered questions."

"Thank you, Detective," said Dunbar. "We have no plans to leave the city."

———

Jenny stepped past the threshold of the psych ward, straightened her shoulders and grinned. A bubble of proud satisfaction swelled in her chest and she fought to keep from jumping in the air and whooping in delight. Later. She'd celebrate later. Right now, she wanted as much distance from this loathsome environment as she could manage.

A brisk walk brought her to the bank of elevators. The tiger roused and informed her Zach stood inside the car ascending to her floor.

Her joy fled, replaced by anger at the man's duplicity. The tiger growled his disagreement, but Jenny ignored his opinion and embraced righteous indignation.

When the door slid open, Jenny stood straight and calm. She studied Zach and permitted the tiger full access to her mind. Together, they reached for Zach's thoughts.

The insight this exercise yielded amazed her. Zach shielded

his mind carefully, but Jenny/tiger felt distress and guilt leaking around the edges. There was more, a vague impression of hope, and ... longing?

Never mind. Her first attempt at probing another mind had produced information. The achievement thrilled her, but didn't thaw the cold anger Zach's presence triggered. She remained motionless, waited for him to make the first move. The guilt she'd detected confirmed his betrayal. She refused to give him anything else to hold against her.

Zach stepped out of the elevator and grabbed her hand. "Thank God," he said. His hand felt warm, but clammy. It shook slightly. "You're free!"

"No thanks to you!" Snatching her hand back, she wiped it on her pants and moved a few paces away. She turned to face the blank elevator door.

Zach stood rooted to the spot and she felt confusion wash through him, but he reinforced his barrier before the tiger could tell her more.

"What's wrong, Jenny? I've been talking myself hoarse, trying to get the police to release you, but you've managed it on your own." He moved closer, placed a calloused finger under her chin and raised her head, forcing her to meet his eyes. A swift intake of breath betrayed surprise before her tiger could announce it.

"Jenny, I swear, I didn't do this!"

He pulled her into his embrace so swiftly she couldn't resist. The tiger purred contentedly and her anger dissolved. She discovered she didn't want to resist. She wanted to snuggle into Zach's warmth, to marvel at the swift beat of his heart echoing against the ear she pressed to his chest. Distantly, she heard him speak and forced herself to pay attention.

"I'd never hurt you like that. It's not what you think. You're not here because you're psychic, well, not directly..."

She smiled into his shirt. She'd flustered him. Zach Douglass running at the mouth — because of her. She'd heard all she needed, but more importantly, the tiger assured her Zach hadn't betrayed her. Something or someone else worked against them both.

Zach continued to babble and Jenny acted instinctively to stop him. She lifted her face, put her hand behind his neck and drew his mouth down to hers. She'd never kissed a man before, but she understood the mechanics. Her mouth claimed his and the tiger roared with delight. She savored the soft warmth of Zach's lips, so different from his rough, calloused hands.

His mouth opened and she tasted musky sweetness. An electric shock of desire zinged through her body. Oh, God! The sweet excitement she'd experienced during movie love scenes paled in comparison to reality.

She pulled her body closer to his and thrilled when his arms tightened around her, protecting her back, claiming her body. She marveled at his quick response to her touch. A rock hard jab near her belly stopped her thoughts and stole her ability to analyze. Unimaginable sensations ... delicious experience ... bursts of desire ... she existed to merge with Zach Douglass.

Uncle Andrew's voice hit her like a shower of icy needles. "You two might want to save that for a more appropriate venue."

## 14

Jenny tore herself from Zach's arms, and the sudden deprivation of her warm, supple body staggered him. His world reeled from the impact of her kiss. The intensity of his physical reaction forced him to question his sanity.

Maybe Kate had a point. His reactions to Jenny did seem excessive, especially for a man supposedly mourning the loss of a fiancée and life-long friend.

Zach's emotions rotated through a rapid-fire sequence: guilt, exhilaration, shame, lust, excitement, embarrassment, intoxication, rage, enchantment. A thirty-year-old man shouldn't experience such confusion, not over a single kiss. He settled on irritation and rounded on Dunbar.

"Keep your quips to yourself, Dunbar. Let's get out of here."

Andrew Dunbar responded with a wicked grin and crossed the hall to gather his niece in his arms. "I know it's not as exciting as Zach's hug," he said in a stage whisper, "but I'm glad to see you, too."

Jenny laughed, face flushed, eyes bright. Zach scowled.

Dunbar released Jenny and asked, "How did this happen? I

followed Zach up here to rescue you, and here you are, free as a bird waiting for an elevator. What happened?"

Pride and satisfaction glowed in Jenny's eyes. "I remembered that I'm not a child anymore," she said. The elevator doors opened and the three of them stepped into the car. "I demanded to be released. The nurse wasn't happy, but she found a doctor to check me out and he couldn't find any legitimate reason to hold me." She grinned at Dunbar's amazed expression. "Assuming the police don't stop me, I'm a free woman."

"They won't bother you," Zach said. "That's what Andrew and I have been doing — convincing the detective he didn't have any reason to detain you."

She nodded, reached for Zach's hand and entwined her fingers with his. "Thank you. I'm sorry I doubted you."

He squeezed her hand and smiled. "A natural conclusion. One I'm glad we cleared up."

Dunbar cleared his throat and Jenny broke eye contact with Zach. She blushed a deep scarlet and stared up at the lighted numbers counting down their descent to the lobby.

Zach controlled his thoughts and reined in his exaltation. Jenny had kissed him. The attraction was mutual.

He scowled at Dunbar to disguise his growing pleasure. He stood quietly, enjoying the contact of her hand in his. He remembered the warm pressure of her lips, the hungry passion and the way she ignited a deep desire to drag her into the nearest janitorial closet, rip her clothes off and...

He cut off that line of thought, disgusted with himself. She continued to hold his hand — trusting as a lamb — while he molested her in his mind.

He scowled and his fingers twitched in her grasp. She glanced up and smiled a shy, secret smile. He looked away, jaw tightening. What did she know about the firestorm she'd kindled in his heart? Not a damned thing. She'd kissed him. She hadn't offered to bear his children. He had to pull himself together.

He tightened his shields and concentrated on Dunbar. Jenny's uncle stared at the elevator panels, seemingly relaxed and untroubled. Zach exhaled a long, slow breath, unsure whether to curse or praise Dunbar's restraining presence.

*Easy,* the quiet Angie-echo whispered across his roiling emotions. *You ... Jenny ... good.*

A knot of tension in his shoulders released and he glanced down at Jenny.

*Yes,* said the quiet voice. *Yes.*

Warmth expanded through his chest. Jenny had kissed him. Attraction existed on both sides. That was enough for now.

The elevator stopped and Dunbar held the door for Jenny and Zach. They walked through the lobby in silence, Jenny still clinging to Zach. When they reached the door, Dunbar reached for Jenny's free hand, patted it and tucked it firmly in the crook of his arm. "Let's get out of here," he said.

Jenny nodded, released Zach's hand with a regretful smile and followed her uncle from the hospital.

---

The next few days passed in relative calm. Zach shadowed Jenny diligently during working hours, but maintained a discreet distance.

Jenny appreciated his presence and his obvious concern for her mental and physical well-being, but his equally obvious efforts to keep her at a distance disturbed her. Her growing comfort with the tiger made her acutely aware of the wall Zach had erected. She wanted nothing so much as to batter that wall to pieces, but she knew, even if she could, the action would be morally and ethically wrong. Besides, she wasn't at all convinced she had the strength to pull it off. She contented herself with reliving the passion of their first kiss, a passion she knew he had shared, despite his current reserve.

With the assistance of her tiger, Jenny finished a complete translation of the rune book. She still had misgivings about committing the instructions to a language readily available to the masses, but Zach assured her the manuscript would be well protected. He intended to drive it to the Institute in Seattle himself, where the brightest psychics and parapsychologists in the country would study it. He expected to leave in the morning and Jenny feared she'd never see him again. The rune book had brought them together and now it seemed it would separate them forever.

She had just finished printing a copy of the manuscript when Zach walked into her office.

"I burned the translation onto a CD for you," she said, looking up from her computer screen. "Do you want me to make another back-up before I erase the file from my hard drive?"

Zach dropped into the client chair across from her. "Yes, that's a good idea. I'm glad to hear you're purging the information from your computer."

She nodded and added a second CD to her drive. "I won't feel comfortable 'til this document is out of our office." She hit a few keys and leaned back in her chair. "Are you sure it'll be safe in Seattle?"

"I'm sure. The Institute is accustomed to dealing with this sort of thing." He studied her for a moment, his expression veiled and brooding. "Come to Seattle with me, Jenny."

Her breath caught and her pulse raced. "What?"

He expelled the breath he'd been holding and ran a hand through his hair. When he dropped his hand, his emotions spilled across his barrier. She recognized intense anxiety over the pending separation.

"You heard me," he said. "I asked you to come to Seattle with me. I'd like you to see the Institute, meet some of the staff." His gaze challenged her and he spoke his next words distinctly. "You need to understand that you're not alone in your abilities. You're not a freak."

She swallowed a sudden lump in her throat and stared at her computer screen. Anything was preferable to meeting his eyes. "I can't, Zach. You know I can't." She removed the newly created CD, placed it in a jewel case and typed the command to purge the translation from her hard drive. "Detective Anderson told me not to leave town."

Zach jumped to his feet and paced her small office. "I'll talk to Anderson, explain it's just a weekend trip." He stopped and dropped both hands onto the surface of her oak desk. "If Anderson gives the okay, will you come?"

"I don't know, Zach. Let me talk to Uncle Andrew, see what he thinks."

She was stalling and she knew it. Her heart had nearly jumped from her chest at his suggestion. Her reaction frightened her. She desperately wanted to go away with Zach, far away, possibly forever, but not just to be put on display at an institute for weirdoes. He was suggesting a business trip, not a romantic weekend for two.

He started to leave, but turned back and rounded her desk. He grabbed her hand and pulled her to her feet.

"Please, Jenny. I can't explain it, but I can't be separated from you."

His barrier cracked and anxiety, desire and uncertainty washed over her. The strength of his feelings overwhelmed her. The room swam in front of her eyes. She wanted to sit down, put her head between her knees, but Zach swept her into his arms. He enveloped her with warmth and strength, and her world righted.

"Yes, Zach," she whispered from the safety of his embrace. "You arrange it and I'll go with you."

His arms tightened around her and he exhaled into her hair. She felt his relief as distinctly as she did the knot tying her stomach into a writhing mass. How would she guard her heart, alone in Seattle with Zach?

# 15

The day stretched ahead of Jenny, a strange mixture of anxiety and boredom. Trapped in a car with Zach, the atmosphere between them too thick for easy conversation — four hours of strained silence lay between them and the Institute in Seattle. Four hours. She thought of the psych ward where she'd recently spent a few hours and relaxed a little. Four hours of discomfort was nothing compared to the horror she had recently escaped.

Her tiger stopped pacing, lowered his massive bulk to lounge comfortably, and anxiety drained from her mind. He might be relaxed, but he remained alert, aware of currents beyond the limitations of Jenny's physical senses.

*Talk to him,* the tiger growled. *He longs to hear your voice. You are more important to him than he knows. Your destinies lie together.*

"Have you worked for the Institute long?"

The words were out of Jenny's mouth before she knew she intended to speak. Her tiger had tired of waiting.

Zach glanced sideways at her, surprise etched on his rugged face. "Five years," he said. "I started there right after I finished my fellowship in Scotland."

"That's right," she said, "I remember you saying you'd studied in Scotland. I've never been there, but Uncle Andrew loves to tell me about The Homeland." She smiled, remembering her uncle's fondness for their ancestral home.

"Yes, I understand the feeling. There's something about the British Isles that stirs the blood of a Celt," Zach said, smiling ahead at the highway, "even Celts as far removed as we are. I loved my time in Scotland, felt very at home."

She studied his profile, enjoying the opportunity to stare with impunity. "If you liked it so much, why did you leave?"

He chanced a quick look at her and focused back on his driving. "Because I'm an American. Scotland is my heritage, and the University of Edinburgh gave me an education in a field I couldn't study in the U.S., but this is my home. America is my future."

They rode in silence for a few minutes, but the quality of the silence had changed. An easy camaraderie replaced the earlier tension. Her tiger had been wise to push her into speech. She must learn to trust his instincts.

She smiled at the thought. Trust the tiger she'd dedicated so many years to banishing from her mind.

"What's funny?"

She glanced up to find Zach watching her. Her skin flushed. "You'd better watch the road, mister."

His gaze returned to the highway. "Really, Jenny. What were you thinking about just then?"

Maybe because he looked at the road instead of at her, or maybe because her tiger prodded, but Jenny discovered she wanted to talk to Zach about her gift.

"It's silly," she said, "but it just occurred to me. I've spent the last eleven years trying to push my tiger out of my mind and now I'm discovering he's an asset." She glanced out the side window of the car and watched the trees whip past ... like the last eleven years had done. She'd come full circle, back to the beginning, trying to get a handle on her psychic powers, on the tiger in her mind.

"You see your gift as a tiger." He made it sound matter of fact, completely natural. "That's an interesting insight."

"You think so?"

"Tigers are dangerous animals. Is your gift a danger to you, or others?"

"Oh, cool," she said dryly. "I'm trapped in a car with a psychologist intent on analyzing me. Help me, Obi Wan Kenobi. You're the only one who can."

Zach barked with laughter and, after a moment, Jenny joined him. When the hilarity subsided, Jenny wiped her eyes and leaned her head against the back of the seat. "Honestly, Zach," she said, "I don't know what to think. I'd just started dealing with this ... well, this tiger, when my parents died."

When she didn't continue, Zach filled the gap. "Then came the nightmare of the psyche ward," he said quietly, "and you decided it was smarter to push your gift into a dark corner and pretend it didn't exist."

She closed her eyes. "Yes, that's it exactly. I couldn't do it, not really. But I learned I could use meditation and rigid emotional control to keep the tiger at bay. At least, I could when I was awake."

"Ah," he said, "you started having dreams. I bet they were doozies. Do you remember any of them?"

The strap of her seat belt suddenly felt too restrictive. She fidgeted in her seat, adjusted the shoulder belt's angle, squirmed again, but couldn't escape the question he'd asked. She stilled and decided to answer honestly.

"I'd done a pretty good job of burying them, until I met you."

"Me?" He swung his gaze toward her and then forced it back to the highway. "What did I do?"

"I started dreaming about you when I was sixteen." She drew her braid over her shoulder and fiddled with the loose hairs at its end. "I recognized you the moment you walked through the door."

Zach gripped the steering wheel so tightly his knuckles whitened, but his voice remained calm. "What kind of dreams?"

She smiled and drew the end of her braid across her cheek. "Nothing bad. Childish dreams, really. You tamed the tiger and rescued me from danger." She froze, the fingers holding her braid stalled in mid-air. "You *are* the tiger tamer," she said in a hushed voice. "He recognized you, too."

Zach frowned, but kept his eyes focused straight ahead. "I don't understand. How am I a tiger tamer?"

Jenny dropped her braid and wiped sweaty palms on her black chino slacks, leaving a dark damp streak. "You have to understand, I fought my tiger constantly, trying to keep him in his corner, but then, that first day when you walked into the office, he broke out. He's refused to allow me to corner him since." She paused and licked her lips. "But whenever you're around, he's calm. He even purrs." She cast a sidelong glance at Zach. "I've never known him to purr before. I think he knows you can help us learn to live together, help me learn to trust my abilities."

Zach signaled, checked his mirrors and pulled to the side of the highway. He parked the car, unclasped his seat belt and turned to face her.

"You're seriously telling me that you recognized me from your dreams? You'd seen my face before we met?"

Jenny shrank back against the car door. The expression in Zach's eyes frightened her, and her tiger slept — probably a good sign, but she wanted, no needed his insight, his extrasensory information right now.

"I'm sorry, Zach," she said, unable to look away from his

relentless brown eyes, "I didn't mean to offend you. But you did ask about my dreams."

"Offend me?" He rolled his eyes skyward. "The woman tells me I'm her knight in shining armor and then apologizes for offending me."

He leaned across the center console. "I'm not offended, Jenny, I'm astounded. You're amazing."

His mouth descended and she met his lips instinctively, inexorably, with a surety of destiny fulfilled. She strained against her seat belt and longed to be free, to throw herself wholly into the branding fire of his embrace.

She inhaled his fragrance. The combination of aftershave, soap and hint of sweat tantalized. She loved his smell, but he tasted even better. She opened her mouth. His tongue flicked inside, accepting the invitation and claiming her more intimately than lips could manage.

Oh, God, his hands! Not content to merely hold her, he gave them free rein to roam over her body. His right hand found the firm mound of her breast, captive below layers of modest clothing. She moaned into his mouth.

His touch ignited a firestorm of sensations. Her flesh couldn't contain such heat without melting into a puddle on the seat. Then again, maybe the melting process had already begun. Her insides had gone all liquid and sloshy. Her secret area, the part of herself she knew so little about ... well, the dampness of her panties testified to his liquefying effect. Zach had awakened a woman's desire and Jenny ached to explore its mysterious ramifications.

The kiss ended too soon. Zach pulled away from her, removing the support of mouth and hands, and Jenny blessed the seat belt's support. Her muscles no longer functioned properly. He trailed a finger down her cheek, opened his door and sprang out.

"I need some air," he called over his shoulder and slammed the door.

Her brain struggled against a fog of dazed confusion, but she noted the spot where he sprinted into the lurking forest a few yards from the highway. Instinct and desire screamed at her to leap from the car and follow him, but the cautious comptroller commanded she remain in her seat belt's safe, if sterile, embrace.

They had parked on a busy highway. They couldn't both run off into the woods and do who knew what while their car sat deserted on the roadside. What if they emerged from the forest and discovered it missing, towed away?

If that happened, they'd walk, she told her sensible self. She unbuckled the seat belt with fingers rendered momentarily uncooperative and climbed from the car on unsteady legs. Focused on the tree he'd disappeared behind, she drew a deep breath and sent up a quick prayer to any and all gods who protected the innocent — and the foolish.

Jenny knew exactly what she hoped and expected would happen if she followed Zach into the woods. Her heart pounded with anticipation. Fumbling for her purse, she extracted the condom she'd stowed hopefully in her wallet over a year ago. Stuffing the foil-wrapped square in her pocket, she sprinted for the woods.

Jennifer Elaine Murdoch had been a virgin long enough. The man of her dreams waited behind the screen of trees and she was anxious to discover if sex with Zach Douglass could possibly be more mind-blowing than his kisses.

## 16

Zach leaned against the trunk of a massive cedar, hands in his pockets, head bowed. Jenny stopped the moment she caught sight of him, before he noticed her presence. She prodded her tiger, desperate to know whether or not to approach, but her tiger merely gave her a reproachful stare, closed his eyes and rolled over.

She fingered the end of her braid. He hadn't seen her yet. She could return to the car, pretend she'd never left. But, if she did, this opportunity, this golden moment, would be lost forever. She reached for her tiger one last time. He refused to budge.

*Fine,* she thought. *Be that way.*

Squaring her shoulders and flipping her braid behind her shoulder, Jenny wound her way among the trees to claim the man she desired.

A twig crunched beneath her leather loafer and Zach looked up. Despair clouded his eyes. She stopped. Desire was one thing, despair, quite another.

"I'm sorry," she said, stepping backward. "I misread the situation."

He pushed away from the tree and held out his hand to her. "No, Jenny. Don't go."

"Are you sure? You look so sad."

"I'm confused. I admit it." He closed the distance between them and placed his hands on her shoulders. "I can't figure out how I can be so attracted to you when a few weeks ago Angie and I were planning our wedding." He closed his eyes and pulled her into his arms. "But confusion aside, I want you. Desperately."

His voice, low and gruff, rasped across her nerves and left her itchy for more.

"I'm sorry Angie died, Zach," she whispered. "She was a kind and capable woman." She pulled out of his embrace and gazed into his eyes. "But I'm here now and I've been waiting for you all my life. Don't push me away."

Zach pulled her back into the circle of his arms and completed their connection with another kiss. Unlike the hungry desire and passionate combustion of the first two kisses, this one began in compassion, two souls touching with care and consideration, each aware of the other's fragility. But it didn't end there.

Jenny deepened the kiss, opened her mouth and herself to him. Her tiger stretched, and with his aid, she sent Zach a surge of willingness, sent him the sure and certain knowledge she desired his advances. Zach's answering burst of passion smothered every lingering doubt.

Afterwards, she wondered how they'd managed to shed their clothes without separating. She couldn't remember losing contact with his strong, limber body for a single moment. Yet here she lay, in a patch of redwood sorrel without a stitch of clothing between them.

He rolled away from her, smiled wickedly and held up the

foil wrapped square she'd been clutching when she arrived. "Want to do the honors?"

Her gaze leapt to his erection and her eyes widened. She licked her lips and reached for the condom. "What do I do?"

His delicious, sexy laugh rumbled through their forest bower and she shivered, feverish with excitement. "It's not exactly rocket science. Open the packet, put it on the tip of my cock and roll it down."

She matched actions to his words, marveling at her own daring. She was touching a man's privates. Oh, God! She lay naked in the woods fondling Zach Douglass's cock.

A nervous giggle escaped and her hand trembled as she rolled the paper-thin latex down the length of his warm, firm shaft. His breath caught and her grip tightened in response.

"Oh, yeah," he breathed, and then his hands were on her. Tiny droplets of fire seared her flesh each place his fingers touched, burning away the last vestiges of petty fear and self-consciousness. She moaned, closed her eyes, and concentrated on the exquisite sensations his hands evoked as they explored her body.

He circled her right nipple with a rough fingertip and she shivered in delight. Flames spread from the firm bud in molten waves. When he licked the same nipple, a shock of ice froze the fire and her loins clenched. She grabbed his hair and dragged his head closer to her breast, and he responded by sucking — hard.

Jenny dug her nails into his back, relaxed and ran her hands along his ribs. Awareness vacillated between hard muscles beneath her hands and the hot, moist mouth on her breast. The schism of perception drove her mad, but what an ecstatic, erotic madness. She arched up, driving her breast more firmly against his ravaging tongue, while her hands continued their sensual exploration of his bare skin.

When her roving fingers found his rock-hard shaft, Zach's mouth stilled. Unsure of herself, she pulled her hand away. He raised his head from her breast, stared into her eyes and guided her hand back to his erection.

"Don't stop," he whispered and thrust his tongue into her open mouth.

She gripped him tightly, amazed and a little frightened by her boldness. She wavered between sensations, the warm, pulsing hardness filling her hand and the insistent, restless tongue filling her mouth. God! Her heart already battered against her chest and he'd barely begun to love her. What if she didn't survive her first sexual experience?

Her mind ceased to function. She existed to experience each delirious moment. She'd never be able to catalogue every caress, every lick of his tongue, each nip of his teeth, but she'd always remember the moment he filled her completely, the glorious instant when their bodies merged.

He settled himself between her legs and filled her with one swift thrust. Pain eclipsed her pleasure. She gasped and stilled, but his voracious tongue continued to ravage her swollen mouth and she responded to the dual probe with an unconscious adjustment of her hips. He settled more deeply inside her and the ache subsided. She cried out, but the sound was lost in his kiss.

Had he consciously used his tongue to distract her from the discomfort of his initial thrust? Intended or not, his technique mastered her fear. He filled her so thoroughly, so totally — ecstasy threatened to overwhelm her. She fought to stay with him, to ride the swelling crest to its unknown peak. Every thrust of his powerful hips pushed her closer to sanity's edge. A heady adrenaline rush urged her to let go, to fly beyond the boundaries of mundane reality.

They fell into an ancient rocking motion, echoing the waves

breaking on the shore. Each penetration surged deeper, each retraction elicited a clutching gasp. *No, don't move away! Come in, come closer, be one with me!*

She clung to him, opened to him, accepted him. She'd never guessed she could fit so perfectly, resonate so completely with another being. Her hands clenched around his back, moved up to bury themselves in his hair, down to grab the firm curve of his buttocks.

*Deeper, go deeper!* She urged him on with lips, hands, mind and soul. *Yes, yes, YES!*

She screamed his name, legs firmly entwined around his, hands grasping his bottom, satin sheath milking his shaft spasmodically. They climaxed together.

Always, together...

...but his mind remained shielded. A small annoyance in an abundance of bliss.

———

Zach rolled away from Jenny's seductive softness, afraid he'd crush her with the dead weight of his spent body. Exhaustion blocked his ability to think, but his arm stole back and pulled her close to him. He needed her touch, longed to lower his shields and meet her tiger, but the Angie-echo chided him each time he thought of relaxing his barrier and he had no desire to chat with Angie in this intimate venue.

Jenny lay curled in the crook of his arm, the controlled young woman who'd stolen his heart. He had wondered what she'd be like when her control broke. Now he knew and the knowledge amazed him. She fit him perfectly. Her body seemed designed to mold to his. She'd matched him fire for fire, passion for passion. Nothing withheld, nothing reserved in case things didn't work out. She took his breath away.

He'd guessed her to be a virgin even before his first thrust had confirmed the truth. Her life had given her little opportunity to be otherwise. But she'd ridden the wave of passion all the way to shore. She'd accompanied him willingly to orgasm. A single cry at his initial penetration had been her only testimony to unfamiliarity with the ways of the flesh.

Zach felt her stir and turned his head to nuzzle her hair. He smiled, lifted a lethargic hand to push a stray wisp from her face. Her hair strained to escape its confining braid.

"When will you let your hair down, Jenny?" He murmured the words more for his own amusement than to elicit an answer.

"I thought I just did," she whispered, mischief and light filling her voice. She ran her hand through the dark curls on his broad chest.

He laughed. "I'm thoroughly convinced of your natural abilities." He kissed her forehead, tasted the salt tang of sweat and breathed in the sweet scent of their lovemaking. "I meant when will you unbraid your hair? I want to run my hands through it."

She sat up, drew the thick braid over her shoulder and provided a provocative show of unbinding her long, dark hair.

God, what beauty! Her hair shone mahogany against the cream of her breasts. Her nipples, rosy and taut from his kisses, peeked out through the shining tresses. His gaze followed the flow of hair down and rested on the soft roundness of hips and belly. Her long legs, tucked beneath her, hid the prize of her femininity.

The desire to run his hands through her hair paled and he hardened yet again. He pulled himself to her and buried his head in her lap. A swift intake of breath signaled surprise and a glorious fall of hair shrouded his shoulders. She stroked his back. His tongue found the honey he'd been seeking and a tremor of delight shuddered through his soul. She cried out with pleasure, and exultation exploded in his chest. Her hands locked his head in place and she toppled back into the sorrel.

His erection ached with the need to seek her soft, sleek wetness, but he held himself back. He wanted to savor her this time. He stretched his body full length between her legs, his head nestled at their apex. She writhed, her questing fingers finding only the top of his head. She clenched his hair in shaking fists.

He drove his tongue deep inside her silken temple and she arched her back. Small, quick, flicks of his tongue had her writhing in the fragrant sorrel. Her movements drove him to the edge of ejaculation. He'd fly apart if he didn't bury himself inside her warmth.

He wrenched his mouth from her womanhood and licked his way up her body. When he kissed her mouth, she stilled, startled by her first taste of their combined passion. He raised his head and stared into wide, golden eyes.

"What are you waiting for?" she whispered, her voice husky and low.

"I want to watch you, this time." He rolled onto his back in the springy green vegetation and his erection speared the air. "Sit on me."

Jenny straddled his body and lowered herself onto his hard shaft. Zach groaned with relief and reached up to cup her breasts in grateful hands. She raised her hands to her hair and arched back. Pulling her hair up, she released it to cascade over the backs of his hands and wrists. She closed her eyes and rocked her hips, sliding up and down, back and forth, over his erection.

Zach kneaded her breasts, hypnotized by her erotic movements until the sheer seduction of her body coupling with his own numbed his mind. He closed his eyes, dropped his hands to her waist and held on while she rode him to ecstasy.

After they climaxed, she fell forward onto his chest and would have rolled off if he hadn't held her in place. They fell asleep with him still inside, flaccid now, but infinitely satisfied.

---

Zach startled awake. What had he been thinking? Falling asleep and leaving her unprotected! Now that she'd thoroughly satisfied his pecker, his rational mind took over with a vengeance. They had to dress and get back to the car.

"Jenny." He said her name quietly, gently shaking her. "Jenny, we have to get up now."

He definitely had to get out of this position. Jiggling her warm, soft body while she slept on top of him: big mistake. He fought to keep his wits about him. He couldn't succumb to her willing inexperience.

"Come on, sweetheart, wake up." If he'd only had the sense to let her slip off of him when she'd wanted to, he could have dressed quickly and carried her to the car.

Yeah, right. He'd been thoroughly sensible right after the most mind-blowing sex he'd ever experienced.

Okay, no biggie. He could do this. He tightened his arms around her and prepared to roll over. She chose that moment to open a sleepy eye.

"Again?" she asked with a yawn. "Don't you ever get tired?"

The soft petulance in her voice undid him. He burst out laughing, hugging her close while he laughed uncontrollably.

"What's so funny?"

"Nothing, sweetheart," he said when he could talk again. "I'm just a little off balance." He slapped her rump. "Get up, Jen. We need to get dressed and find out if we still have a car."

She scrambled to her feet and stared toward the highway. "Do you really think it might be gone?"

She looked magnificent, standing there nude, poised to run to the car's rescue. He almost pulled her back down into the sorrel again. Instead, he forced himself to his feet and began to gather his scattered clothing.

"Nah. If the police had found it, they'd've found us, too."

That got her attention. She dived for her clothes and wiggled provocatively into them. He shook his head, turned away from the enticing sight and pulled on his jeans and polo shirt.

When they were both dressed, they headed to the car. Jenny got the giggles as they walked, but Zach kept moving, afraid to stop again under those enchanted trees. Once they were safely in the car, he turned to her.

"What're you laughing at?"

"Us," she said, trying to put a sober expression on her face. "I can just see us walking into the Institute like this. My hair's in snarls and you've got grass stains on your shirt."

He glanced down at his bedraggled shirt and grinned. She had a point. They were a mess. He reached over and patted her knee.

"Don't worry about it. We'll stop by my apartment and clean up before we put in an appearance at the Institute." He gave her a stern look and pointed a finger at her. "But you have to promise to stay out of my sight until you're fully dressed and ready to go." He broke into another grin. "Otherwise, we'll never make it past my bed."

She bowed her head and a shield of hair hid her face. "Speaking of beds, do I still have to get a motel room tonight?"

"Not if you don't want to. I'm willing to share." The idea of having her in his bed all night slammed him in the gut. He hardened instantly. Man, she was killing him.

He put the car in gear and eased onto the highway, away from the seductive lure of soft, green sorrel.

# 17

"Zach, I'm concerned about you." James Towne stood in the center of his fifth floor office, hands in the pockets of a perfectly tailored, gray business suit. Zach's debonair employer was in his fifties, physically fit, intelligent and wealthy enough to fund an institute that studied phenomena most scientists considered questionable at best.

"I've been reading Kate's report," he continued. "She seems to think you've lost your objectivity where this young woman is concerned."

*Stay calm,* Zach told himself. *He's testing your defenses. Don't give him any ammo.*

Downstairs, Jenny worked with the Institute's best trainer to test and quantify her gift. Zach had taken the opportunity to check in with James, his employer and friend.

"Kate oversteps herself," Zach replied, keeping his voice cool and evenly modulated.

James nodded and ushered him to the sitting area. A large, black leather sofa invited Zach to rest. He chose a wingback chair instead.

"Tell me about Miss Murdoch," James said.

Zach sat forward and tried to keep the excitement from his voice. "She's the most amazing untrained talent I've ever met. She's terrified of her gift, and given her history, who can blame her? Even so, she's already showing signs of being able to control it."

He couldn't sit still, couldn't hold his emotions in check and keep his body at rest at the same time. He jumped up and paced the midnight blue carpet. James' gaze followed him across the room.

"The first manifestation took me completely by surprise" he said. "Like she disappeared inside her own head and this other entity spoke to me. She calls it her tiger. That's how she thinks of her gift, a tiger stalking her mind."

Zach stopped in front of a wide picture window that perfectly framed the Space Needle in the distance. He wanted to confide in James, confess his infatuation with Jenny, discuss the deep confusion the attraction caused, but James already thought he had lost his objectivity. He didn't want to confirm his friend's suspicions.

"What is it, Zach? What's troubling you about this girl?"

He'd hesitated too long. James' psychic gift had kicked in. Zach engaged every shield he'd learned in his years of training and turned to face him.

"She knew me, James," he said quietly. "Before we ever met, she knew me."

Zach recognized the laser-edged look in James' eyes and knew his employer's sensors had all engaged. "Explain, please."

"She's been dreaming of my face since her teen years." Zach scrubbed his forehead with his hand. "You read my report on her history?"

James nodded.

"During her confinement, she made every effort to suppress her gift. It worked during the day, but at night, the sight emerged in dreams." He buried his fists in his pockets and stalked back to the seating area.

"I don't know what it means and I don't think she does either, but she recognized me the first time we met." Zach dropped into the burgundy wing-backed chair again.

"And you're convinced she's telling the truth?" James asked.

Zach sat silent for a moment, considering his next words. "I think Jenny is capable of lying superbly. She had to have perfected that skill in order to survive her incarceration." He leaned forward and stared directly into James' eyes. "But, yes, I believe she's telling me the truth about this." He looked away, steeled himself and made eye contact again. "I can't explain it, James, but I'm connected to her. It's like I've been waiting for her all my life."

"You realize that last statement supports Kate's contention about your objectivity."

"Yes," he admitted, "but I still think Kate's overstepped her bounds. You and Kate are worried about my objectivity. Well, I'm worried about Kate's lack of restraint. You know she called the police when all we needed was a bottle of smelling salts."

James waved Zach's comment away. "She was concerned. She overreacted."

"Her overreaction landed Jenny in a locked psych unit. She could have pushed Jenny over the edge with that stunt."

"If Ms. Murdoch is so fragile and unstable, perhaps Kate's suspicions are well-founded."

"For God's sake, James." He balled his fists and thrust them in his trouser pockets. "Jenny's not involved in this crime. It's a physical impossibility."

"I suppose you have evidence to support that opinion?"

"As a matter of fact, I do."

"Well, then, what are you waiting for? Let's hear it."

Zach exhaled sharply and ran his hands through his hair. He'd managed to talk himself into a corner.

"Fine," he said. "The murderer used a sex rite. She not only disemboweled her victim, she used power from their sexual activities to fuel the rite. Jenny couldn't have completed the rite — she was a virgin until this morning."

"And you know that how?"

Zach scowled at the older man. "What? Did you want me to video our encounter? I had sex with her before we made it to Seattle. Trust me. I deflowered her. I'm not so naïve that I can't recognize a virgin's first sexual experience."

"I see," said James, turning away from Zach and walking to the window. "Well, that settles it. I'm taking you off this investigation. You've completely compromised your ability to think logically where this young woman is concerned. I'll assign another team immediately."

"Fine. Assign another team. Do whatever you feel is necessary, but do it without me. You take me off this case, I quit."

James wheeled around and glared at Zach. "Don't play power games with me, Zach."

Zach glared back. "This isn't a game and I'm not bluffing. Don't call me on this unless you're willing to watch me walk out that door."

Both men stood perfectly still, staring each other down. After an interminable few moments, James broke the stalemate tapping his fingers against his thigh in a rapid staccato.

Zach exhaled the breath he'd been holding.

"All right. You stay on the case, but so does Kate. Learn to get along or I'll move into my Portland condo and run interference for you."

"I can't ask you to leave your responsibilities..."

"Then find a way to work with Kate."

"Fine."

"Now, brief me on this young woman's translation. How does the rune book affect the case?"

———

Jenny and Zach spent Saturday evening and most of Sunday alternately playing in bed and playing tourist. Zach found it hard to believe Jenny had lived so many years in such close proximity to the great city yet had never visited.

At first he begrudged her the sightseeing, time he'd rather have spent ravishing her delicious body in the comfort of his king-size bed, but when he saw her delight in experiencing the city's variety, he relented and took her to all the standard tourist destinations.

"The next time you come," he said as they descended the Space Needle, "I'll take you to the San Juans. You'll love the ferry ride, and I know a great little bed and breakfast with a private beach." He managed to caress her breast discreetly in the crush of the elevator — a promise of passion to come. Jenny blushed, but moved closer, pressing her body against his.

A business dinner with James was the last thing either of them wanted to waste precious time attending, but Sunday evening found the infatuated couple dressed to the nines and seated at an elaborately appointed dining table in James Towne's posh penthouse apartment.

"More tests, Mr. Towne?" Jenny's gaze challenged him as she raised an exquisite crystal wine glass to her lips.

James raised his own glass, saluted her and said, "More tests, Miss Murdoch, though these are simply games for my own edification." He sipped his wine and replaced the glass on the snowy white tablecloth. "You may, of course, refuse to play."

She and Zach sat in the dining room of James' penthouse. Having spent years in confinement, followed by more years in a tent on an archaeological dig, Jenny was unaccustomed to such grandeur. Polished cherry wood paneled the dining room, while a plush carpet patterned in navy and burgundy covered the floor. Light danced from myriad precisely faceted crystals, which dripped from the chandelier above the opulently appointed table.

But rather than feeling awkward and out of place, peace washed Jenny's mind. Her tiger exuded satiation. His purring satisfaction reminded her of her own contentment after the amazing sex she and Zach had shared in the woods. The tiger liked — no, loved — exerting himself to provide her with psychic insight. It had been quite a weekend: explosive, passionate sexual release for her, coupled with rigorous, exacting psychic stimulation for her tiger. She should be exhausted. Instead, exhilaration pumped through her system.

"Actually," she said, "I'm happy to try new things." Her gaze flitted to Zach, who sat directly across the table from her, and returned to his employer.

James sat at the head of the table, the undisputed lord and master of his domain. He nodded, stood and held out a hand to Jenny. "Let's retire to the library where we can relax. Zach, you're coming, of course?"

The silk of her strapless evening gown fell gracefully into place around Jenny's legs as she stood and stepped away from her chair to grasp James' hand. She'd felt ridiculous purchasing the frothy red confection earlier in the day, but she enjoyed the appreciative glances it elicited from Zach and James. Heightened sexual awareness allowed her to identify the rasp in Zach's voice when he responded to James' question. Or maybe her tiger provided the insight. However it came, she recognized possessive jealousy and thrilled to know she caused it.

"I'm certainly not leaving her alone with you," Zach said. His dark eyes sparkled with challenge.

James laughed.

The sound skipped lightly across the room's furnishings and enticed Jenny's tiger. He sat alert, sniffing the air for stray tidbits of information.

James tucked Jenny's right hand into the crook of his arm. She held out her left to Zach. She and James stood quietly, waiting for Zach to round the table and complete the trio. With both men securely linked to Jenny, James led the way into the library. Fortunately, the wide double doors were thrown open. No male dominance displays were required to enter the room.

The library spoke to Jenny of a different kind of wealth, an intellectual prosperity she both understood and appreciated. Uncle Andrew would love this room.

The same plush carpet from the dining room extended here, but the similarity ended with the flooring. Gleaming mahogany shelves lined the walls and overflowed with books of every description.

Jenny freed herself from both men and flew to the shelves. She caressed leather-bound volumes lined beside colorful paperbacks. Some bindings were obviously hand-sewn, while others boasted machine work. The lettering on the spines ranged from gold leaf to simple printer's type to ornate calligraphy. What treasures!

She whirled to take in the rest of the room. True to the tasteful luxury of the dining room, the library coddled the body while it indulged the mind. Comfortable overstuffed chairs reposed beside a capacious couch and luxuriated in front of a large, stone hearth. Each seat boasted its own reading lamp. In the heart of the room stood the *pièce de résistance*, a massive library table accompanied by matching chairs. A large book lay on a dais at the center of the table. Jenny knew without question that this volume was James' greatest treasure.

Without taking her gaze from the massive tome, Jenny asked, "What book is that, Mr. Towne?"

"Does it call you, my dear?"

Jenny tore her attention from the book and focused on the men. James studied her, eyes shining with delight. Zach glanced from James to Jenny, confusion etched on his rugged face.

"What's going on here? James?"

Zach looked uneasy and Jenny longed to reassure him, but the book on the table held her enthralled. If she moved, she would go to it, not Zach.

James nodded and the spell dissipated. He smiled at Zach. "Everything's fine, my friend." His gaze returned to Jenny. "You've brought me an exceedingly rare gift in this young woman." When he spoke again, his words were for her alone. "You may inspect it, if you like."

She flew to the table, reaching the huge book before his words died. Her tiger paced, tail switching, waiting for her fingers to touch the book. She laid her hand on its cover, guilty pleasure flooding her soul as gloveless fingers caressed the leather. Knowledge poured into her mind at first contact. Her tiger roared. Power and light emanated from him, passed through her mind and out her mouth.

"Have a care, James Towne. This gramarye is ancient and related to the one causing the trouble in Portland. Its secrets are not for untrained minds. The powers contained herein require consummate skill to control. You should monitor who has access to this volume."

Jenny shuddered, blinked once and blushed. "I'm sorry, Mr. Towne. I don't know what came over me, speaking to you like that."

James and Zach crossed the room and joined Jenny at the reading table. Zach placed a protective arm around her waist while James reached out and stroked the gramarye's open page.

"Don't concern yourself, Ms. Murdoch. I seem to remember Zach mentioning you think of your gift as a tiger?" He paused and she confirmed his words with a nod. "I believe your tiger just addressed me directly. How fascinating."

Zach eyed the book uncomfortably. "Let's move back to the sitting area," he suggested, exerting gentle pressure on Jenny's waist. He guided her to the large leather couch. They settled themselves on its cushioned surface, and he turned his attention to James.

"See what I mean?"

"Was that similar to what happened the first time her power manifested in your presence?" James asked and then turned to Jenny. "Excuse me, my dear, for talking about you in your presence, but I don't think you were conscious during the other episode."

Jenny's eyes widened. "I had another episode?"

Zach nodded. "You fainted the first time you examined the rune book, remember? Your tiger spoke to me then." He turned to face James. "Different words, but similar intent — don't meddle with what you don't understand."

James took up residence in an overstuffed chair beside the large hearth. He steepled his fingers and frowned into space. "I've never felt the need to have the gramarye translated," he said, nodding toward the library table. "I can feel its power, of course, but I've been content to hold it as a museum piece. Perhaps my attitude has been negligent. What do you think, Jenny? May I call you Jenny?"

She smiled and said, "Yes, certainly, Mr. Towne."

"Here, now. If we're going to be on a first name basis, you must call me James."

"All right ... James. To answer your question, I don't think it's imperative for you to know what's in the gramarye. I don't have any sense of foreboding or evil about it, not like the one Zach brought to me. I'd be delighted to do the translation, of course, but I think it's safe to have it on display. I'm sure my tiger is correct, though. You'll want to monitor who has access to it."

He nodded. "Very well. We'll leave the mystery of the gramarye alone for the moment." He settled back into his chair and relaxed his hands on the plush arms. "Now, I wonder if you'd indulge my curiosity for a few moments."

She felt Zach stiffen beside her and answered with a cautious, "Of course."

James must have felt Zach's discomfort, because he smiled and said, "Relax, Zach. Miss Murdoch is perfectly safe with me. Now, Jenny. I'd like you to be at ease. Rest your body, but extend your mind. What can you tell me about myself?" He paused and then chuckled. "And you can dispense with the rich and good-looking part. That's a given."

Jenny laughed, and Zach relaxed enough to release her hand and place his arm across the back of the couch behind her shoulders. She closed her eyes and imagined stroking her tiger's magnificent head. Opening her eyes, she turned their combined focus upon Zach's employer and received an abundance of impressions.

"You're very open, James." She turned their eyes on Zach, whose defenses remained tight. "Not like some people, I know."

Refocusing on James, she considered which pieces of information to present to him. She had no desire to embarrass him in front of Zach.

"You are an adept clairvoyant. You fund the Institute to debunk charlatans, but mainly you desire to find other psychics like yourself. You want to know you are not alone, and in meeting this basic need, you give others a place to belong. But most urgently," she said, "I feel your pain. Someone close to you has died and you're filled with guilt and regret. You feel responsible for her death and overwhelmed because you failed to adequately express your love. She died without knowing how you felt."

# 18

J ames' face turned pasty white.

Jenny froze. Oh, God. She'd been too explicit in her revelations. Well, it had been a fairly open-ended question. A psychic himself, surely James knew better than to ask for information he didn't want.

"James," Jenny said. "Mr. Towne? Are you okay, sir?"

Her question met stunned silence. Her tiger curled up and closed his eyes, but the emotional eddies swirling around the room continued to bombard her mind.

"I'm sorry, sir," she said. "I didn't mean to offend you."

James silenced her with a gesture and closed his eyes. When he opened them again, color flooded his face.

"Nonsense," he said. "I asked the question, didn't I? It's just that, well, in all the years I've been asking potential candidates for information about myself ... well, let's just say, no one has ever captured my motivations, my emotions with quite such ... um ... clarity."

James rose and walked to the gramarye. Jenny and Zach adjusted their positions on the couch to keep him in sight. The older man rested his hands lightly on the massive book's surface.

"I like to think I'm a philanthropist," he said, staring at the ancient manuscript, "but you're quite correct. At their base, my motivations are purely selfish." He sighed and closed his eyes again, visibly shaken. "I'd prefer not to discuss the other matter."

"To hell with what you'd prefer," Zach said, his voice tight with anger. "Was she talking about Angie? Did you and Angie have something going on? Something you conveniently forgot to tell me?"

James' eyes flew open, defiance blazing from their dark blue depths, and he spun to face Zach. "Watch yourself, Zach. I don't owe you any explanations."

"The hell you don't!" Zach jumped to his feet and paced to stand opposite James, the gramarye table between them. "She was my fiancée and my best friend. We were planning our wedding, for God's sake."

"Right," said James. His jaw tightened, making his words clipped and rough. "She had agreed to marry you, so I kept my feelings to myself." He broke off, scoured his face with his hand and started again, his voice bleak. "And now she's dead, because I sent her to Portland. I sent her to investigate a case and she was murdered because of it."

Zach deflated and sank into the chair beside the gramarye table. "I'm sorry, James," he said. "Fighting with you over 'might-have-beens' won't solve anything."

James dropped into the chair across the table from Zach. "It doesn't matter," he murmured. "She's gone. Neither one of us will get to love her or watch over her. For what it's worth, I never told her. I respected you both too much to interfere with your relationship." He smiled weakly. "Besides, she loved you. She would've done anything for you."

Jenny rose from the couch and walked over to take her place

on the third side of the table. "Is that why you're so tightly shielded?" she asked Zach, glancing at James for confirmation. "Did Angie do something to you, at the end? Try to protect you somehow?"

Both men turned to face her. Zach looked guarded and chagrined at the same time, while James exuded puzzlement.

Jenny stammered, unsure if she'd stumbled into a topic not discussed among the gifted. "I mean, I've been wondering why Zach is so impervious to my gift." She glanced at Zach apologetically. "I haven't been trying to read your mind or anything, but I've never been able to pick up more than the occasional whisper of your emotions."

"Yes," said James, nodding slightly and turning an appraising gaze on the man across the table. "You do have new shields in place. I noticed them earlier." He paused and glanced back at Jenny, eyebrows raised in curiosity. "Frankly, I assumed he was shielding to protect you."

Jenny started in surprise. "Protect me? From what?" She shook her head and said, "No, he's been shielded since I first met him."

They turned their attention to Zach, who glanced between them, an uneasy expression on his face. "Okay. Yeah. I'm shielded and I stay shielded. Always. Something happened after Angie died. Something I still don't believe, so I've kept it to myself."

James' eyes narrowed and he leaned toward Zach. "Spill it."

Zach shifted in his chair. His gaze darted from James to Jenny and landed on his fingers, which he drummed on the table's polished surface. "Every time I drop my shields, I hear Angie's voice insisting I'm in danger." He raised his chin and squared his shoulders. "She's not exactly haunting me, but she's still with me. Still watching out for me." His gaze hardened and he added, "And no, I'm not imagining it and I'm definitely not insane."

"You're in contact with Angie's ghost? Has she told you who did this, who's responsible for her death?"

"No. I've wondered about that, but she only comments on two things, Jenny and my shields." He stopped drumming, jumped to his feet and paced around the room. "Those were the last two things she said to me before she died. Get your shields up and find Jenny Murdoch."

He came to rest opposite James and leaned forward, hands braced on the table. "Her echo or ghost, or whatever, seems to be stuck on those two topics. They're the only things she comments on. *Keep yourself shielded and trust Jenny. She'll help you heal.*"

"Angie sent you to me?" Jenny's voice caught on the words. "She thinks I'll help you heal?" Soft, but slightly hysterical laughter escaped her and she clamped a hand over her mouth. "I'm sorry," she said through her fingers, "but everyone's always trying to fix me. I'm the one everyone thinks is wounded."

"I see," said James, his eyes blazing again and directed toward Zach. "Angie was focused on you, trying to protect you." He slammed his hand down on the table and half rose from his chair. "Has it occurred to you that if she'd been paying proper attention, she might have detected the hostile presence? If she hadn't been so consumed with protecting you, getting *you* shielded, giving *you* the book, directing *you* to Jenny, she might have saved herself."

The fire in his eyes died and he collapsed back into his seat. "All she wanted was to protect you and she died because of it."

Ashen-faced, Zach dropped into his chair, folded his arms on the table and bowed his head. A wash of grief and guilt over-whelmed his barriers and lapped at the edges of Jenny's mind.

"She had to protect you, to warn you," Jenny whispered. "She couldn't give you the rune book until your shields were in place. She'd felt its power, knew its evil. She didn't have time to explain, but she knew your mind had to be shielded so you could handle the book without being victimized by it. She couldn't knowingly put you in danger."

Both men raised their heads and stared at her.

"Victimized by it?" asked Zach. "It's dangerous to handle it?"

"What about being close to it?" James asked.

She frowned. "I don't know about proximity. Uncle Andrew's been in the room with it and not been affected, but I've been careful not to let him touch it. My tiger has protected me and Zach has always been tightly shielded."

James frowned. "Don't worry, Jenny. We'll guard the rune book carefully." He stood, walked around the table and offered Zach his hand. "I'm sorry, Zach. I shouldn't have said what I did. Angie wouldn't have been Angie if she hadn't assured your safety. I..."

Zach cut him off. "Forget it," he said. "I've been spouting off like an idiot, too. Angie's dead. We both loved her. Let it go." They shook hands, but a palpable wariness remained in the room.

James released Zach's hand and turned to Jenny. "Earlier you suggested my mind was open to you, while Zach's wasn't. I consciously left my surface thoughts unguarded for you to find." He crossed to her, took her by the elbow and guided her back to the sitting area. "If you'd caught only those, you would have told me things like I find you attractive and I've been enjoying baiting Zach." He glanced apologetically at Zach and continued, "But you chose to ignore those thoughts. You went far deeper, into areas I would've sworn were securely guarded. Your access shocked me. No one's ever slipped past my defenses before." He grimaced. "Your tiger is an exceptionally strong ally."

The next morning Jenny packed for the return to Portland. The bed she'd so enjoyed sharing with Zach mocked her today. Bright sunlight poured across its neatly plumped pillows and smoothed green bedspread. She'd slept poorly last night, huddled on the edge of the mattress, a mournful silence aching between her and Zach. Too many disturbing concepts had been revealed in James' apartment.

Zach loved Angie. His reaction to the revelations about James' emotions had made his feelings entirely too clear. Jenny had no business sleeping with a man who'd recently witnessed the death of the woman he loved. She'd known about his relationship to Angie, but she'd rationalized her actions, ignored the implications. The conversation in James' library had forced her to see reality, not the rosy dream world she'd been living in.

She zipped her suitcase closed and wiped her hands on her jeans. She felt cheap and dirty. If she'd been home, she would have stripped, showered and scrubbed her skin raw.

How could she have been such a fool? How could Zach make love to her with such unrestrained abandon and then react to James with equally passionate jealousy?

She hefted her bag from the bed and rolled it from the bedroom to the front door, glad of an excuse to put some distance between herself and Zach. She didn't want to look at him. More importantly, she didn't want him looking at her. He had to regret what they'd shared. Angie might be dead, but that didn't change his feelings for the woman, didn't mitigate his loss and didn't excuse his betrayal in sleeping with another woman, especially since some form of Angie still existed in his mind.

"Ready?"

Zach had entered the room without her notice.

"Yes," she said, trying — and failing — to put a bright note in her voice. "It's been a lovely weekend, but I'll be glad to get home."

"Yeah," he said. He opened the front door, heaved his paraphernalia through, waited while she rolled her bag into the hall, then glanced back inside, flipped off the lights and sighed. "Yeah, it's been quite an eventful weekend."

He pulled the door closed, locked it and pocketed his keys.

———

Jenny wanted to watch the city recede behind her and experience the nostalgia of the moment to its fullest. Unfortunately, Seattle was one of those sprawling giants that blended from one suburb into another along the interstate. They were an easy sixty miles from its beating heart, before open countryside signaled city's end.

The sky had lost its early morning sparkle and settled into a high overcast when they passed the stretch of highway where they'd parked on Saturday morning. The car whipped past on the way south, but even so, Jenny's pulse quickened and her insides turned mushy. Her tiger knew the spot. If she wished, he could lead her to the exact location — find the bed of crushed sorrel plants she had fertilized with the blood of her sexual awakening.

"You're very quiet," Zach said, breaking the silence and her wistful mood.

Jenny fidgeted with the seat belt's shoulder strap and said, "I was just reviewing the weekend."

"You don't regret ... anything ... do you?"

His voice betrayed apprehension, something she didn't require the tiger's help to understand. She placed a hand on his shoulder.

"Never, Zach."

He glanced at her with shadowed eyes. She caressed his

shoulder and said with absolute certainty, "I'll never regret what I've learned this weekend. Not any of it."

It was true. She'd given Zach her virginity and, whether he loved her or not, she couldn't regret her decision. He had introduced her to passion, helped her quantify her gift and revealed his deep-seated love for a woman who no longer walked this earth — all in the space of two days. She wished the last fact didn't exist, but didn't regret knowing. She'd learned long ago the truth of the adage: *knowledge is power.*

He took one hand off the steering wheel and covered hers where it rested on his shoulder. "I'm glad, Jenny," he whispered. "I'm very glad."

He returned his hand to the steering wheel and she moved hers to her lap. Tonight she'd sleep in her own bed. Alone. Back to reality. She'd traveled through a fairy ring into a place of magic and mystery and she returned with new insight, forever changed. Indelibly marked by the magic she'd experienced. What would the mundane world hold for her now?

The Jennifer Murdoch of a few weeks ago, that poor, frightened, rigidly controlled girl, no longer existed. Now Jenny was a familiar of tigers and a thoroughly bedded woman. Her old life didn't fit anymore. She wished the new one could include a permanent relationship with Zach.

## 19

Jenny returned to work on Tuesday with an altered outlook on life. She approached her assigned tasks with power and confidence. Self-acceptance felt good.

An augmented sense of surroundings notified her of Uncle Andrew's presence in the small office even though her back was turned.

"You must have had quite a weekend," Andrew said. "You seem different this morning, more self-assured."

Jenny closed the file drawer she'd been rummaging through, straightened and turned to face her uncle. "I had an amazing weekend. Zach took me sightseeing. I had dinner at the mansion of an indecently wealthy man, and I endured hours of psychic testing." She walked around her desk and grasped her uncle's hands. "You'll never guess what the tests revealed."

"Really? Well, don't keep me in suspense," he said. "Give it to me straight. I can handle it."

"I know this will be a shock, Uncle," she said. A bubble of pride swelled in her chest. She could say the words, admit to the abilities she'd spent half her life hiding. "I'm psychic and I have the test results to prove it."

She squeezed his hands and smiled at the surprised expression on his weathered face. "I'm clairvoyant. Don't worry. I can't read minds, but I can pick up strong emotions and my interpretations are very reliable."

She leaned back against her desk and gestured him into a chair.

"My clairvoyance also shows a distinct precognitive aspect, which is why I knew about Mom and Dad." Her voice faltered for an instant, but she shrugged and continued. "And I tested positive for PK — psychokinesis. You know, moving things about. I'd never tried that before, so it was pretty erratic at first. I got better, though."

Uncle Andrew whistled. "Now there's a handy skill. Why hire movers? I'll just get my niece to move those heavy boxes with her mind."

Jenny leaned forward and swatted his arm. "I must say, you're taking this awfully well. I expected you to scoff and tell me to get a grip."

He stood and stroked her cheek, eyes eloquent in his sun-lined face. "Jenny, my dear, I may question the scientific method of most parapsychologists, but I wouldn't dream of denying that there are more things at work in the world than we've yet found a way to quantify. Besides," he quipped, patting her shoulder, "if you're happy, you'll work better."

"Well, if you're concerned about productivity, you'd best get out of my office."

Uncle Andrew laughed and strode to the door. He paused on the threshold and glanced over his shoulder. "I'm glad you're happy, Jennifer Elaine."

He left before she could respond.

Detective Anderson stopped by Dunbar Consulting late Tuesday afternoon. At the police officer's first words, Uncle Andrew stormed to the reception area.

"Jenny," he called, striding down the hall, "don't say a word. You don't have to answer any questions. I'll call our attorney."

The homicide detective stood across the reception desk from Jenny. His dark gray trench coat hung on thin shoulders, a wrinkled, ill-fitting sack. The sallow cast to his complexion spoke of too many sleepless nights. He glanced around and scrutinized Dunbar as he approached.

"Relax, Dr. Dunbar," he said. "I'm here to consult with Miss Murdoch, not interrogate her."

Jenny, who hadn't met Detective Anderson at the hospital, waited quietly, observing the two men and assessing the emotion-laden atmosphere they produced.

"You want my help," she said, "but you don't believe I can tell you anything meaningful. And even if I could, you don't think I'm a reliable witness."

Anderson's eyes widened and then narrowed as he absorbed her words. He nodded. "That about sums it up. I don't believe in this hocus-pocus."

"Then why are you here?" Uncle Andrew asked, his voice a low growl. "You're trying to trick her into incriminating herself, aren't you? You might as well admit it, because I'm not letting her say another word to you without our attorney present."

"I already told you. I'm not here to interrogate Ms. Murdoch. The department no longer considers her a viable suspect."

"And what made you change your mind?" Uncle Andrew reminded Jenny of a terrier, unwilling to drop the subject.

Anderson's face reddened and he glanced sideways at Jenny and then quickly away.

"A reliable source provided incontrovertible evidence," he said, glaring at Uncle Andrew. Jenny nudged her tiger toward the surface thoughts behind Anderson's words. The tiger blinked once and dislodged a memory for Jenny's inspection. Her breath caught and her heart pounded.

"Drop it, Uncle Andrew," she said, hoping her cheeks weren't as red as they felt. "Detective Anderson is telling the truth. I'm no longer a suspect."

Zach had seen to that. He'd informed Anderson of their sexual relationship and had assured the police detective of her previous virginity.

Damn the man! She'd rather be a murder suspect than have her intimate relationship flaunted in public.

"Fine," said Uncle Andrew. "I still don't see why you're bothering Jenny."

Anderson thrust his fists deep into the pockets of his rumpled trench coat. "Because we've hit a wall and we need a new direction. The captain thought your niece might be able to tell us something we don't know, get us out of this rut."

"Zach is far more experienced," Jenny said, "and he's already assigned to your case."

"Yeah, but his partner died, remember?" Anderson shrugged. "He's trained to notice things we aren't and he understands the occult crap we found, but his objectivity is compromised. People don't think straight when they're grieving."

*Or when they're screwing a new conquest.*

Jenny blinked and wished she hadn't caught the unspoken end of his thought.

Uncle Andrew's scowl deepened. "Their experienced psychic died," he said, "and you want Jenny to take her place? I don't think so! I'm not letting you put her in that kind of danger."

"What danger?" Anderson looked genuinely puzzled. "The other woman had a heart attack. The coroner did a complete autopsy. Natural causes."

"It's all right, Uncle Andrew," Jenny said. "Angie didn't realize the danger. I do." She patted his hand and he snorted at her. "I'll be careful. I'll even use the psychic shield I've been practicing. Besides, I'm learning to trust my ... gift."

She almost said tiger, but switched words just in time. No need to arouse the good detective's concern about her sanity.

This investigation had brought Zach into Jenny's life. Curiosity welled up inside her. She wanted to know about the crime, wanted to know how the murderer had interpreted the rune book. Moreover, she needed to discover Angie's killer. The psychic's death had wounded Zach and the wound affected Jenny's dreams and desires.

Jenny's tiger flexed his claws and whipped his tail. His eyes glowed with fiery anticipation. A hunt! He crouched, ready to spring into action.

Jenny accepted his counsel. "When do we start, Detective?"

---

Jenny stood frozen in the center of the small room. A uniformed officer, one of three who had accompanied Jenny and Detective Anderson to the scene, drew the blinds closed to prevent the brilliant sunshine from overpowering the scene. A king-size bed rested directly in front of her. Behind, an entertainment center camouflaged a television. To her right, a short hall led to the bathroom and outer door, and to her left, a bank of curtained windows looked out on the city skyline. A man's life had ended in this nondescript hotel room, stripped from him in torture and mutilation.

She stood where his body had lain splayed and vulnerable. The aura of his pain and terror curdled her stomach and she hugged herself, reflexively protecting her core. Through her tiger's eyes, she observed the ritual positioning of his limbs, saw the fine lines of powdered moonstone immobilize him. Horror and fascination warred for dominance in her mind.

His fear and anguish knotted her muscles. Her inability to change his fate slapped her sense of justice. Grief at the loss of his potential to the world dragged at her spirit. At the same time, the ritual intrigued an analytical fraction of her mind. A design drawn in powdered crystals on a hotel room floor had held a strong, fit, adult man captive. The implications made her heart beat faster.

Magic existed. Black magic, a disgusting perversion of power and possibility, but magic, nonetheless.

Her tiger growled and she pulled her attention to his discovery. He illuminated the flux lines running through the room, illustrated the perpetrator's careful choice of location. The unknown woman had taken advantage of the earth's ancient magic to bind her victim. The rune book taught the murderer skills that had been lost in this age of technological wonders.

Jenny shuddered and prayed she'd done right, translating such terrible knowledge into a common tongue.

"Detective Anderson," she called.

The rumpled man emerged from the small bathroom holding a piece of broken tile. He shuffled past the uniform who stood at the corner where the bathroom hall widened into the bedroom.

"Miss Murdoch?"

"You should ask James Towne to run extensive tests on the rune book I translated."

"Who is James Towne and what tests can he run that the department lab can't?"

Jenny turned to face the man. Weariness etched the lines of his face and wariness haunted his eyes. She sighed and dropped onto the edge of the bed.

"James Towne is the founder and principal benefactor of the

Institute for Psychic Research in Seattle. Zach Douglass works for him." She paused, closed her eyes against the memory of the conversation in James' penthouse and reopened them with new resolve. "His people can run specialized tests. They may be able to tell you where the book came from and who had access to it."

"And I care about this book because..."

"Because it taught the murderer how to conduct this ritual."

---

Zach and Kate reached the hotel room door just in time to hear Jenny's pronouncement. Zach's pulse throbbed in his temple. She should have called him. He would have prevented her involvement. Anderson had no business dragging her into the investigation. Jenny had no experience with crime scenes or investigating officers.

"Crap," Kate said, momentarily fragmenting his attention. Zach glanced at her, but his body strained to get inside the room. He needed to protect Jenny.

"What is it?" he asked, forcing himself not to snap with impatience.

"I forgot the lab analysis of the moonstone powder, not to mention all the research I did on the uses of crystal compounds in occult rituals." She dug in her black leather shoulder bag, produced car keys and met his eyes. "I'll get the reports and deliver them to police headquarters, but I hate to leave you stranded. Can you hitch a ride with Anderson or Jenny?"

Zach waved her away, already turning to move into the room. "I'll be fine. Just make sure that information ends up on Anderson's desk."

She disappeared from his radar without another blip. Zach strode into the room, gaze glued to Jenny. His body ached for her. He hadn't realized what a hardship it would be to sleep alone last night. Actually, he hadn't slept at all. He'd tossed and turned. Every time he'd drifted off, his subconscious had awakened him, demanding her soft, pliant body.

*Love her.* Angie's echo whispered in his mind. *Don't hurt her.*

Zach's confidence plummeted and his stride faltered. He halted beside the bathroom door and probed Angie's meaning. Yes, he could see it now. Jenny had been too quiet on the ride home. She'd said she didn't regret their intimacy, but his jealousy over Angie had to have hurt her. God, he'd acted like an idiot, a childish, selfish idiot.

Angie's echo laughed. *Good. Need Jenny ... need you.*

He nodded, squared his shoulders and pushed past a uniformed officer into the main room.

"You gonna come in, Douglass?" Detective Anderson asked in a snarling voice. "Or you just gonna hang there in the doorway with your mouth open?"

At the mention of Zach's name, Jenny whirled to face him. Her gold-tinged eyes sparkled with fire, and Zach's doubts melted in the blaze. He loved her. He belonged to her and she to him, and right now, his instincts screamed at him to protect his mate.

The other men in the room eyed her greedily — a hungry wolf pack with a she-lamb at its center — but Jenny radiated calm competence. Zach stifled a growl, but glanced warily at the men surrounding her.

"What's going on here?" he demanded. "Why did you bring Miss Murdoch to the scene? This room's been cleaned and returned to use. The murder occurred nearly three weeks ago."

"The captain insisted we get a fresh take on the case. We're up against a wall, but we're not going to let this one go," Detective Anderson answered. The man seemed more than tired. He looked haggard and worn.

"But why Jenny?" Zach insisted. "I thought we agreed she had no connection to this case."

Anderson shot him an irritated glance and rolled his shoulders. "Not my idea, so back off."

"I'm fine, Zach," Jenny said, speaking for the first time since he'd entered the room. "I don't know if this room's been used since the murder or not, but the aura is still strong. I've been able to read a lot of what happened here."

She rotated slowly, facing each of the compass points in turn, and the tiny hairs on the back of Zach's neck leapt to attention. She looked so normal, so perfectly mundane in navy slacks, white button-down shirt and deep green cardigan. Her sleekly braided hair and carefully applied make-up combined to display a practical businesswoman.

But she radiated power and every man in the room felt it.

Detective Anderson broke the spell. "She says your boss may be able to shed some light on what happened here."

"James? How?"

"Something about further analysis of the book you found." Anderson flipped open his cell phone and stepped past Zach into the hall.

Zach strode to Jenny's side. "Tell me what you see," he said, "what you've deduced."

She gazed into his eyes, and he had the uncomfortable feeling her tiger was sizing him up, weighing his character. She nodded and the image fled.

"I'm glad you're here, Zach," she said. "These men don't really believe I can tell them anything. They're just humoring a superior officer."

She sighed, and Zach fought the desire to pull her into his arms and hold her close. Instead, he caught her hand and squeezed it. "I understand. Trust your tiger. Tell me everything you sense."

"Did you actually see the body," she asked, "or just photos?"

"Angie and I saw the body. James got us here post haste."

Jenny nodded and pulled her hand free. She pointed to the carpet and described the position and condition of the body in lurid detail. Zach nodded, acknowledging the accuracy of her description, amazed by her detached calm. He glanced up to see the three remaining officers whispering to each other, sending furtive glances at Jenny.

He lowered his barrier enough to pick out the men's comments. She couldn't know these things. Not just by standing in the room where the murder took place. Not after this many days. She described specific details too accurately. She must have seen the corpse. Worse, she must have inflicted the wounds.

Jenny finished speaking and a palpable silence filled the room, one with an edge that grated on Zach's nerves.

Jenny made eye contact with each of the uniforms. "I feel your unease," she said quietly. "Please remember, you brought me here. You asked for my impressions." She nodded at the floor. "I had nothing to do with this. I'm just telling you what the room tells me." Her words fell on stony silence.

Zach nodded to the officers, put his arm around Jenny's waist and led her from the room. Once they reached the hall, he pulled her into a tight embrace. She trembled noticeably, a reaction to the detailed reading she'd just accomplished. "You did a great job in there," he said.

She leaned heavily against his chest, seemingly too exhausted to maintain her balance. "Thanks," she whispered. "I didn't realize it would be so hard, dealing with their suspicion."

He closed his eyes, savoring her softness while trying to shield her from the disquiet of the men standing just inside the door. "You're good," he said, "not just your reading, but the way you handled those men." He laughed, a nervous, uncomfortable sound. "You were scary in there, Jenny, and I'm used to such things. I can't blame those officers. They don't understand."

"Take me home, Zach," she sighed. "I'm exhausted."

He led her to the elevator, cursing Kate for leaving him stranded. No matter. He would manage to find one of Portland's elusive taxis. No way would he subject her to mass transit with her gift in this heightened state.

Detective Anderson stood in front of the elevator, blocking their exit. "We're not finished with her yet, Douglass," he growled.

"Oh, yes, you are," Zach snapped. "She's out on her feet. You brought her here, you have a responsibility to get her safely home."

Anderson's gaze moved from Zach to Jenny's wan face. He considered for a moment, and nodded. "You're right. But I'm going to want to question her about this later."

Jenny roused and flared at Anderson. "I'm not going anywhere. I told your men and I'll tell you; I didn't have anything to do with this. I'm just telling you what the room told me!"

Anderson led them toward the street where his car waited. "You described every detail about the corpse," he said, "but I need you to tell me about the murderer. You told us what the victim looked like, but you didn't describe her. Why is that?"

Jenny slid into the car rear seat and rested her head against the cushioned surface. "I can't describe her. The spell she cast shrouded her. I know you don't believe in magic. I'm not sure I believe in magic, but I didn't see her. Maybe if I'd been able to read the victim..." Her voice trailed away.

Zach closed the car door and wrenched the front passenger door open. "Get in, Anderson," he ordered. "Drive her home. I'm coming along to make sure you don't badger her on the way."

## 20

Jenny spent the next day going about her normal routine, except normal no longer existed. She went to the office and worked on projects her uncle assigned, but they no longer held the fascination they had before Zach walked through her door. Even her noon constitutional — a brisk twenty-minute walk before lunch — left her feeling listless and uninterested. Life was good, but life was flat.

She told herself she was coming down with a new strain of flu, but she knew she lied. She exhibited advanced symptoms, and while the condition wouldn't kill her, she'd carry it to her grave. She had contracted a chronic case of loving Zach Douglass.

Her heart pounded and she wiped clammy hands on her dark green slacks. She had held the knowledge at bay since the trip to Seattle. After all, how could she judge this all-consuming need? She didn't have any prior experience. But this morning, when she woke to find her bed empty, the space Zach should have occupied cool and unrumpled, she'd experienced a breathtaking epiphany. This was more than a sexual fling. This was love.

Everything she'd read said that casual sex was fun, kicky, a rush of excitement. But when it ended, you moved on, eager for the next encounter. Nothing about her attachment to Zach was casual. The idea of moving on, of him holding some other woman the way he had held her, broke her heart. She didn't want any other man. If she couldn't have Zach, she'd live alone, as she always had, and treasure her memories.

He cared for her. She couldn't read his emotions, but his desire to comfort and protect her was obvious. Their physical relationship rocked her world, but his dead fiancée had taken up residence in his head. How healthy could that be?

Yeah, right. The man would be able to fall madly in love with her while having daily séances with Angie. Jenny would trust Zach with her life, but she couldn't imagine him loving her the way she loved him while playing host to Angie's spirit. Her stomach tightened into knots just thinking about it.

Jenny powered down her computer and pulled her purse from the bottom desk drawer. Zach had vouched for her with Detective Anderson, allaying the police officer's doubts by exposing their intimacy. She understood why he'd done it, but the necessity still rankled. Unfortunately, his actions spoke of a desire to protect, not of undying love, and she coveted Zach's love more than anything.

What had she expected? Life had denied her love at every turn. Life had declared her a freak in childhood and had conspired to remove every source of human intimacy from her world. She'd been isolated with her tiger and she'd responded by imprisoning him in a vain attempt to be *normal*.

If Zach couldn't release the past and accept her love, she'd still have her tiger — but this time, she'd choose a different path. This time she intended to embrace her tiger. She could have insight, a measure of power, and she would earn Zach's respect. Jennifer Elaine Murdoch would channel all her pent up emotion into her tiger, and the two of them would become a formidable team. They would defeat this killer and anyone else who tried to warp psychic energy to debased ends.

Jenny's eyes shone with determination. Bring on the perverts. Murdoch and Tiger were open for business!

---

Zach strode through the door the next morning and Jenny's determination stumbled. "Good morning, Jenny." His predatory gaze traveled the length of her body and her heart raced, excitedly rushing blood through her veins. Her skin tingled and her face flamed. Selfless service to mankind sounded great — when she was alone. Her mind understood the fine distinction between love and lust, but her body quivered in anticipation of his touch.

Zach prowled around her office like a big cat. Lithe and powerful, he brimmed with constrained sensuality. Her knees weakened and resolve liquefied. The man reeked masculinity. A primeval god returned to life to sport with mortal women once more. And he'd chosen her.

She sighed, the rush of breath echoing the rush of blood through her veins. Mere mortals didn't demand love from a god. A mortal woman accepted his favor, drank every drop of exhilaration and subsisted on its sustaining energy for the rest of her life.

He didn't love her, still clung to Angie. So be it. He wanted her. Lust might not provide the nourishment her soul required to flourish, but she would survive. She'd savor the ecstasy of his passion and treasure the memory for eternity.

"Come away with me, Jenny."

His softly spoken words echoed her fantasy so closely she wondered if she'd imagined them.

"What?" She stared at him, her face hot with embarrassment. She must look like a frightened fawn. She wanted to appear serene, a woman of the world.

He leaned closer and she inhaled the heady combination of spicy aftershave and musky male. "Come away with me," he whispered again. "Things are too complicated here. I want you to myself, at least for the weekend."

She licked her lips, worked to push air past frozen vocal chords. "What ... what about the police? Your investigation?"

A hint of annoyance flickered across his features. "I'll deal with all that, but I need a reason to bother. You haven't said you'll come."

Jenny stared into the chocolate pools of his eyes. Warm, liquid depths enticed her to take the plunge, to join him.

"Of course, I'll come," she said. As if she'd had a choice.

She broke the seductive eye contact. He reached out and tucked a strand of hair behind her ear. He straightened, his manner suddenly brisk.

"Good. I'll make all the arrangements. We'll have dinner in town and then drive out to the coast. Can you be ready by six?"

Jenny nodded, unable to resist the gale force of his masculinity. Why would she want to resist when those winds were blowing her to a romantic weekend with the man she'd dreamed of all her life?

She stood, walked around her desk and said, "I'll be ready."

*I'll always be ready*, she thought, standing on tiptoe to kiss his provocative mouth. She'd intended to give him a soft peck on the lips, but his growl of desire, the swift heat of his mouth opening to devour hers, the steel of his arms embracing her, turned her intentions upside down. A momentary instinct to struggle died under an avalanche of pleasure. Jenny pressed herself against Zach and gave in to the sensory overload of passion. Sensations too numerous to catalog rushed to seal a bargain for intoxicating adventure.

Zach released her lips suddenly and pushed her away, but continued to hold her arms in a vise-like grip. A very good thing. His kiss had turned her legs to rubber and she needed his support to stay upright.

"I've got to go." He said the words, but his body stayed rooted to the floor. His hands continued to grasp her arms. He shuddered, released her and dropped his hands to his sides. After a moment, he strode to the door where he turned and studied her a final time.

"I'll see you tonight," he said.

"I'll be ready," she repeated, her fingers tracing the imprint of his mouth on her lips. She laughed.

*Who am I kidding?* she thought with giddy embarrassment. *I'm ready right now!*

## 21

Twilight had purpled into night when Zach and Jenny climbed the steep steps from the two-car parking area to the front door of the beach house. An odd little dwelling, the cabin perched on a ridge between an inland lake and the vast Pacific Ocean. The cabin appeared to be the normal board and batten construction of all its neighbors, but peering through the wide picture window showed Jenny interior walls formed by logs of varying sizes. She wondered why anyone would bother to frame over a log house.

Her thoughts snapped back to the matter at hand when the front door creaked open. A petite, wizened woman with flowing grey hair peered at them over small rectangular glasses.

"Yes? What can I do for you?" Her voice sounded thin and reedy, but the tone spoke of confidence.

"Diane Clearwater?"

Zach's deep bass thrilled Jenny, but the slight tremor at its core caused a small frown to crease her forehead. She wondered what had him worried.

"Yes," said the woman. "I'm Diane."

"Ms. Clearwater," Zach said, the tremor smoothing out. "I'm

Zach Douglass and this is my friend and colleague, Jenny Murdoch." He paused to shake her proffered hand and waited while the women shook hands as well. "James Towne gave me your name. I'm a parapsychologist employed by his institute. James suggested you might be able to help me with an on-going investigation."

"James sent you? Well, then by all means, please, come in."

Diane stepped away from the door and they followed her into a well-lit living room. To their left, a flight of half-log steps rose to the second floor, but the lower room remained open all the way to the rafters. A massive stone fireplace stood in the middle of the wall to their right and all the seating centered on the source of warmth. Everything, from hardwood floors to the green plaid sofa, sang of well-loved, well-cared for utility.

"Please, make yourselves at home. May I offer you coffee? Tea, perhaps?"

Zach spoke for them both. "Thank you, Ms. Clearwater. We're fine."

Jenny settled into a threadbare corduroy armchair, while Zach perched on the edge of the green plaid sofa. Diane chose a maple rocking chair with a patchwork cushion.

"Tell me," Diane said quietly when all were settled. "How can I be of help?"

Silence stretched. Jenny spoke for the first time. "I don't know why we're here, Ms. Clearwater, but Zach's reticence suggests it has something to do with me. May I ask, what is your particular talent?"

Diane laughed, a cool bubbling sound, like water tripping over stones. "My talent is unique, quite different from what folks generally think of as mind reading. You might say I read souls." She paused, eyes sparkling with amusement while Jenny digested the unexpected comment. "I see stains on people's psyches and I know which ones are valid and which are self-imposed."

Diane turned to study Zach. "Did you bring this young woman here for a reading?"

He nodded and glanced quickly at Jenny, a tinge of red coloring his sun-darkened cheeks. "It's not what you think, Jenny," he said. "I know you had nothing to do with the ... well with the matter I'm investigating."

Jenny favored him with an aloof expression, but inwardly she huddled against her tiger for support.

"Well, whatever you're concerned about, don't be." Diane turned her attention from Zach to Jenny. "The only stain I see on your soul, my dear, is strictly self-imposed."

She leaned forward in the rocking chair, her gaze capturing Jenny's. "I don't know what you blame yourself for — my talent doesn't give me details — but stop it. Whatever happened, it wasn't your fault. You didn't cause it. Your talent didn't cause it. You are innocent. If anything, you're a victim of circumstance."

Jenny's eyes filled with tears. The log walls surrounding her pressed in. She couldn't breathe.

She wrenched her gaze from Diane's, stood and ran from the house. She didn't stop until she stood on the darkening beach, where the boom of the waves pounded Diane's words from her mind. She walked mechanically along the surf-hardened sand and allowed the white noise of the restless ocean to cleanse her soul.

---

When Jenny ran from the room, Zach sprang to his feet to follow. Diane stopped him. Her agility surprised him. So did her words.

"She'll be fine. Give her a few minutes," she said, catching the sleeve of his jacket in her gnarled fingers. "Tell me, Mr. Douglass. Why did you bring her here?"

He sank back onto the sofa and scrubbed his hand across his forehead. "Because she needs to allow herself to heal, and I didn't know how to accomplish the task." He blew out a long breath and met Diane's gaze. "Perhaps I made a mistake."

Diane shook her head. "There's more," she said quietly. "Tell me why you chose me."

Zach's eyes narrowed. "I told you. James recommended you."

Diane shrugged. "Like I told Jenny, I can't read your mind, but I can see that you're not being completely honest with me." She cocked her head, as if to gain a new perspective on his soul. "You have a remarkably clear aura, Zach. You're an honest man at the core. Be honest now. Why did you really bring Jenny here?"

"Because I love her, but my fiancée died and is, I don't know, haunting me, I guess you'd say. Angie says I belong with Jenny, that she'll help me and that I have to help her heal. Only I don't know how to heal her. I'm a psychologist. I should be able to help her, but I can't seem to think straight when I'm around Jenny. I love her too much."

The words tumbled from his mouth, unaided by conscious thought. Once started, he couldn't seem to stop himself, or maybe he didn't want to stop. Maybe he needed to say the words, out loud, in front of a witness.

He loved Jenny. There. He'd said the fateful words. He loved Jenny.

A bubble of relief expanded his chest. He wanted to shout the news before he popped. He exhaled a tremendous sigh and tension drained from his body. He didn't have to hold himself in check anymore. He loved Jenny. If he could say it to himself, to Diane, he could say it to Jenny.

Diane brought him back to reality with a slight tug of the

jacket sleeve. When he focused on her, he found her face wreathed in a bright smile.

"Feels good to be honest with yourself, doesn't it?" She laughed again, then sobered. "I can't help you with the ghost of your fiancée, though if she's urging you into this young woman's arms, I doubt she'll be a lasting problem. About Jenny's need to heal, I think you did right to bring her to me. Her conscience is crystal clear except for the unwarranted blame she's heaped on herself. She needs absolution. I hope she'll accept it from me."

Diane released his arm, stood and walked to the window facing the ever-changing ocean. "Now that you've found your own honesty, go help Jenny find hers."

Zach raced out the door and down the steps before Diane could turn to wish him well.

---

Zach peered through the deepening dark. When he caught sight of the lone figure standing motionless in the soft moonlight, he ran to join her. She'd put a lot of distance between them while Diane held him back, forced him to face his motivations. When he caught up with the woman he loved, his breath came in short, ragged gasps. He forced himself to stand quietly beside her while his breathing regulated and the surf roiled inches from their toes.

Jenny spoke first. "Don't feel bad, Zach," she said, pitching her voice to carry above the pounding surf. "I already knew you didn't love me, but I didn't think you still suspected me of murder."

"I didn't and I don't," he said. "I didn't bring you here about the murder investigation. I brought you here to face your past."

"My past?" she asked, peering at him through the gloom. "Why would you do that?"

"Because Angie said I had to help you heal," he said, tearing his gaze from her pearly face and staring instead at the white foam shimmering a few feet away. "I couldn't think of any other way to convince you that what happened to your parents wasn't your fault."

"Angie," she said, unmistakable bitterness roughening her voice. She turned and walked back along the beach, noting where his footprints had obliterated hers.

Zach kept pace with her. "From the first, Angie's been telling me two things: keep my shields up and trust you. She knows me better than I know myself."

"I didn't like it," Jenny said quietly, "that you could take me to bed while still clinging to Angie, but I understood." She stopped and stared toward the majestic waves. "Sex is just a physical release. It's got nothing to do with love."

Zach grabbed her shoulders and turned her to face him. "It's got everything to do with love," he said, "and I'm not clinging to Angie. She's just with me. I didn't ask her to stay, but she was my best friend and I'm not trying to get rid of her either. Not until she's ready to go." He scowled at Jenny for a moment and then pulled her into a tight embrace. "I didn't follow you out here to argue about Angie. I followed you to tell you I love you. I've been trying not to, but I can't stop myself. I love you."

She twisted in his arms and rested her cheek on his chest. Her body trembled and a sudden shower of tears dampened his shirt. He waited — held her close, sheltered her from the salt-laden ocean breeze, and waited.

"What's wrong with me?" she said finally. "Why did you try so hard not to love me? Why are you disappointed that you do?" She gulped a lungful of air and buried her face deeper in his shirt, crying harder now.

Zach didn't move a muscle. When he gained a measure of

control, he burrowed a hand beneath her chin and forced her head up to meet his gaze.

"There's nothing wrong with you, Jenny, and I'm not disappointed. I'm amazed." He gently kissed her upturned face and led her to a piece of driftwood just visible in the moon's new light. He sat down and pulled her onto his lap.

"When I first met you," he said, choosing his words carefully, "I was mourning the loss of my fiancée, my best friend." He stopped and rubbed his chin across the crown of her head. "I loved Angie, but not the way I love you. I realize the difference now. I cherished Angie as a friend, but I never felt the passion for her that you inspire. She and I could've had a fine marriage, but she deserved more. She deserved James. Unfortunately, she never knew about his love and that's my fault. Maybe guilt made me react so jealously at James' townhouse." He swallowed hard. "I mean, I prevented her from discovering the kind of passion I have with you."

Jenny sniffled, and he tightened his embrace. "I avoided admitting I love you, not because I'm disappointed in you, but because I thought I was being disloyal to Angie."

"Oh, Zach..."

"Hush, I need to say this out loud." He pushed her back so he could see her face. "I love you, Jennifer Elaine Murdoch. You, not Angie. Angie was a wonderful woman and my closest friend, but you, you're my destiny. And what's more, Angie knows it and so does your tiger. Angie's been nagging me, insisting I belong with you, and I'm willing to bet your tiger has been doing something similar."

He closed his eyes and rested his forehead against hers. After a moment, he raised his head and gathered her close to his chest once more. Jenny snuggled in, playing with a button on his shirt.

"I know you didn't have anything to do with the murder in Portland," he said. A sudden tightening in his chest made his voice sound hoarse, gruffer than he'd intended. "But even if you did, even if you'd butchered that poor man, you'd still be the woman I love and I'd give my life to save you."

Jenny froze. Her body tensed in his arms and she stopped fiddling with his button. After a moment, she relaxed, tipped back her head and stretched her free arm up to pull his lips to hers.

Her breath warmed the chill from his lips before her soft mouth molded to his. Her pliancy sent a thrill of pleasure racing along his nerves. A faint scent of lavender tussled with the ocean's salt tang. He liked the contradiction.

She opened her mouth. Her tongue darted between his lips and he responded instantly, claiming the proffered gift. Gods, she tasted sweeter than the chocolate bar they'd shared in the car. His tongue dipped into her mouth and his brain short-circuited. Conscious thought ceased, his world contracted to the pleasure of delicious warmth melting into his mouth and hands.

She broke away and he almost growled. He stifled the sound and gazed into her tawny eyes. The fire smoldering in those golden depths made his heart hammer.

"Did you have a room reserved for us somewhere?" she asked in a husky purr.

He nodded, temporarily devoid of speech.

"Then let's check in." She smiled and a mischievous sparkle lit her face. "I think we have quite a bit more honesty to explore."

---

Jenny nestled into the warm hollow their lovemaking had created in the bedding. Zach's arms wrapped her in comfort and she enjoyed the sensation of her sweaty skin pressed against the coarse springiness of his chest hair. Deep, sonorous breath whispered past her ear. She liked the rhythm of his soft snores.

Wonderful. Life was wonderful. She loved this man and he loved her. And sex with Zach ... well, mind-bending barely skimmed the surface. She stroked his arm where it rested beneath her naked breasts. So strong, yet so gentle when he loved her.

Safe in his arms, her mind drifted back to Diane's words. Knowing Zach loved her had strengthened her. She could afford to explore the wound Diane had exposed.

The tiger prowled her inner landscape. His tail switched and his eyes burned with a baleful fire. She wanted to soothe him, but knew she couldn't. Not yet. Not until she faced her guilty demon.

Diane had proclaimed her innocent, but the only absolution that mattered would come from herself.

*Look back. Remember.*

Her heart raced and she fidgeted against Zach's solid presence.

*Be still. Look back. You're an adult now. Remember with an adult's understanding. Put the child to bed. Don't see with a twelve-year-old's fears. Remember with an intelligent, dispassionate, adult researcher's calm presence of mind.*

Jenny ran through her calming meditations, and when her stampeding heart beat quietly again, she closed her eyes, snuggled closer to Zach's warmth and forced herself to look at the terrifying, long-buried memories.

Twelve years old. A tall, gangly girl. All arms and legs and not a hint of breasts. Despite her awkward appearance, she had been content with herself, in a manner pre-teens seldom are. She had held a secret gift deep within, and it gave her hope and confidence and a sense of who she would become.

Her life had held its share of challenges. Her mother, for one.

Deirdre Murdoch loved her daughter fiercely, but worried about Jenny's future. Raised among the legends of her Celtic ancestors, Deirdre recognized the signs of *second sight* and feared for her child's sanity. Though her instincts told her it was hopeless, Deirdre tried to purge the gift from Jenny's mind. She refused to listen to Jenny's predictions and chided the child for spouting nonsense. But deep inside, Deirdre believed every word Jenny spoke.

Looking back, remembering nuances of conversations, the adult Jenny recognized her mother's fear. She nodded to herself and accepted her mother's love.

*Stop avoiding it. Look at the pivotal memory.*

Jenny tensed, consciously relaxed and opened the memory of the day her parents died. She'd had a vision, a terrifying scene of leaping flames and agonized faces. A vivid nightmare complete with screams and heat and the stench of burning flesh. She'd learned to keep such things to herself. Her mother didn't want to hear about her unnatural thoughts. However, the final detail of her vision had sent her racing to her father's study, heedless of the need to prepare for school ...

"Dad, you have to listen to me!" Jenny skidded to a halt in front of her father's large oak desk. "This is super important!"

Kenneth Murdoch raised his eyes to his daughter's face and pushed back from his desk. He held out his arms and Jenny threw herself into them. He drew his woman-child onto his lap and stroked her long, dark hair.

"Tell me, love," he murmured. "What's got you all upset this early in the morning?"

"It was awful, Daddy," she whispered. "I saw a fire. People died. And, Daddy..." She swallowed convulsively, bile rising in her throat. "You and Momma ... you were there. Oh, Daddy, promise me you'll stay home tonight!"

Kenneth patted her back and whispered soothing phrases in

her ear. When she calmed, he squeezed her gently and prodded her off his lap. He stood beside her, his strong arm around her shoulders.

"We can't live in fear, Jenny, my love." He kissed her forehead and guided her to the front door. "I promise I'll take your vision seriously, but I won't be ruled by fear."

Kenneth kissed the tip of her nose, helped her gather her things and sent her out the door to the waiting car pool. "Put this out of your mind. It's my problem now."

Jenny ran down the steps and off to school. When she arrived home that afternoon, her parents were out. Her favorite sitter waited for her with tickets to the hottest new movie and a note from her dad.

*Jenny, my love, after considering your premonition, your mother and I have changed our plans. We're still going out, but we'll be dining with Ed Corelli at his home instead of the restaurant we'd planned to visit. Have fun with Elaine.*

*Love, Dad.*

Her father's final note had nearly driven Jenny insane. Ed Corelli's penthouse apartment went up in flames that night — with all occupants trapped inside.

---

Zach woke to find Jenny sobbing into her pillow. He rolled her over and cradled her against his chest. Hot tears bathed his skin. He kissed the top of her head and waited out the storm. When the squall passed, he helped her sit up and handed her a tissue. She wiped her eyes and blew her nose. Her breathing eased and he drew her back into the circle of his arms.

"My love-making wasn't that bad, was it?"

She slapped his arm half-heartedly and relaxed against his

chest. Round, firm breasts rubbed against his forearm when she moved. She smelled enticing.

"Stop fishing for compliments," she said. "You know perfectly well I could stay in bed with you forever."

The way she wiggled when she talked made it difficult for him to concentrate. Something important had happened. He needed to focus on her mind. He needed space.

Gently, he moved away, pulling the sheets up to cover her seductive body and replace his warmth. When he'd gained a safe distance, he took her hand and said, "Now, tell me what's troubling you."

She gravitated toward the comfort of his arms, but he held up a cautionary hand.

"Sweetheart, I can't think straight with you in my arms — naked." He tried to look stern, but only succeeded in feeling foolish. "If you need me to hold you while we talk, then we've got to get out of bed and get some clothes on."

Jenny froze, eyes wide. She blushed, pulled the sheet higher on her chest and leaned back against her pillows.

"I'm sorry," she whispered, "I didn't realize..."

Zach leaned close and silenced her with a gentle kiss. When he sat back, a neutral expanse of bed separated them.

"I love you and I want to help. Now, tell me what's wrong."

She took a deep breath and twisted a wad of sheet between her fingers. "You were sleeping and I felt safe." She glanced at him and then refocused on the knot of cotton. "You know, secure, maybe for the first time since I was little. Anyway, I decided to think about what Diane said, about me not being guilty, about letting go of old stuff."

She stopped twisting the sheet and smoothed it flat against her thigh. When she lifted her eyes to meet his gaze, the sorrow and vulnerability he read there made him ache to hold her close, protect her; promise her nothing would ever hurt her again. He clenched his fists under the sheet and kept silent.

"Diane was wrong," she whispered. "It was my fault. My gift killed them. I didn't cause the fire by seeing it in advance, but they changed their plans because of what I'd seen. I sent them into those flames." She closed her eyes and rested her head on the padded headboard. "I warned Dad, and because he honored my vision, he cancelled one dinner reservation and accepted another. If I'd kept quiet, they'd still be alive."

To hell with his discomfort. She needed to be held. Zach pulled Jenny into his arms and crushed her trembling body to his chest.

"You can't know that for certain, Jenny," he said quietly. "Hush now. Listen to me. I've seen a lot of weird stuff in this business, and if your tiger said they would die in a fire that night, then they might have been fated to die by fire no matter where they were."

"But, if that's true," she said, her voice thick with misery, "then I killed Mr. Corelli and his staff."

Zach sighed and relaxed the pressure of his arms. He stroked her hair, releasing a soft whiff of lavender. "Jenny, my love, we can play the what-if game until the sun grows cold and we still won't have a definitive answer. The important thing is our intention. Did you intend to cause your parents pain or suffering?"

She stiffened. "No, of course not!"

"Did you tell your father your vision intending to terrify him into changing his plans so you could get something you wanted?"

"No, but..."

"Did your father scold you for bothering him with your nonsense?"

"No, but..."

"Think, Jenny. What did your father say to you? The last time he actually spoke to you, what did he say?"

She buried her head against his chest and whispered, "He told me not to worry about it, that it was his problem."

She pulled away from him and raised her eyes to meet his. She swallowed, and Zach found his attention riveted on the workings of the small muscles in her throat, a throat he longed to kiss. He wrenched his gaze away and focused on her eyes, which brimmed with tears.

"Daddy didn't believe he'd die, but he told me I wasn't responsible. He said he'd deal with whatever happened."

Her voice broke, and so did Zach's resolve. He pulled her into his arms and covered her face with kisses. The salt of her tears mingled with the scent of lavender.

"Of course you weren't responsible," he murmured. "Your parents loved you. How could they not?"

He paused to kiss her mouth deeply, his tongue dancing seductively with hers. When he pulled gently away, he stroked her face, following the contours of her cheeks and lips with his thumb.

"They wouldn't want you to blame yourself. You know that, don't you?"

She nodded. He couldn't call her beautiful at the moment, not with streaming eyes, puffy face and bright red nose, and yet, her vulnerability made her all the more desirable. He engulfed her in a hungry embrace, determined to replace the mute misery in her eyes with life-affirming passion.

## 22

J enny accepted her absolution and met the fire of her
lover's passion with a fervor born of newfound determination to live her life fully. Her parents had died long
ago and her vision might or might not have played a
role. But Zach had spoken truly: she'd never know the answer
for certain. What she knew without doubt was her parents' love.
Her father had honored her gift by changing his plans. The time
had come for her to honor her tiger as well.

Zach deepened his kiss and she lost the thread of her ratio-
nalizations. His vitality demanded her complete attention. He
ripped the sheet from her body and ran his calloused hands
over her exposed flesh while his mouth devoured hers. Nimble
fingers paused to caress her breasts and pinch her nipples to
erection, and she gasped against his invading tongue.

His cock stabbed between her legs and moved with unerring
accuracy toward her velvet wetness. She raked his back with her
fingernails and opened her thighs, removing the last obstacle
between his rock-hard blade and her soft, moist sheath. Zach
plunged full-length into her willing body. She absorbed the

shock of his thrust and echoed the primal shudder that shook his powerful torso.

Ah, bliss! He was back where he belonged, safely, securely, sheltered within her sex. Tremors shuddered through her body, goading him to deeper thrusts. He released her lips and locked his gaze on hers. His hips pulled back, gathered strength for a still deeper plunge. She clenched tighter, unwilling to lose his stretching fullness, even momentarily. He pounded down, drove her hips into the mattress. She adjusted to the stroke, tilted her pelvis and took him deeper yet, seeking the final, ultimate touch, the sweet spot that would drive her over the edge and release the flood building just beyond her reach.

They strove together; Zach driving into her relentlessly; Jenny enticing him, grabbing and pulling him ever deeper. Almost there! Their sweat-slick bodies struggled to merge, to press together so firmly they ceased to be separate beings. Jenny panted and twisted her hips, grinding herself harder onto his shaft. One more thrust, just a little harder, higher ... almost there ... a little deeper ... push for it ... PUSH ...

"Yes!" she screamed and exploded in ecstasy. His body bucked and she grabbed his buttocks, locking him inside. She shivered, fulfilled and exhausted, while she convulsed rapidly around his shaft, claiming every drop of his tribute. At last, her spasms quieted and exhaustion claimed her.

Jenny lay pressed under the weight of Zach's inert body. She could barely breathe, but refused to ask him to move. Their bodies had labored fervently for a shattering orgasm. Exhaustion tasted sweet.

At last Zach roused himself enough to mitigate his crushing weight. He propped himself on his elbows and their gazes locked.

"I want you in my bed for the rest of my life," he said, leaning forward to nibble her lower lip. "Marry me, Jenny."

So simple, so concise, so exquisitely perfect. Not a question to be answered, nor a command to be obeyed, but a truth to be acknowledged. Jenny flushed and her body shivered through one final, convulsive tightening on his still-embedded shaft.

"Yes," she said, and rolled with him onto their sides to settle into a comfortable tangle of arms and legs for a secure, satisfied sleep.

---

Zach and Jenny spent a glorious summer weekend exploring the Oregon Coast. They drove the coast highway, stopping at nearly every roadside park to walk white sand beaches, scramble over huge basalt boulders and watch sea lions and harbor seals bask on small rocky islands among the breakers.

The sun shone benevolently and the sea breeze whipped Jenny's long hair into a mass of tangles, but she didn't care. Zach loved watching her hair stream in the wind and protested every time she tried to control it in her usual thick braid.

"I wanted to unbraid your hair the first time I saw you," he said while she dressed the first morning after their decision to marry. "Leave it loose for me, just for today."

She might never braid it again, not if the wind-blown mess pleased Zach. She leaned back against the seat headrest and studied his profile while he guided the car south along the twisting coast highway.

Zach loved her. They were going to be married. This man, whose face had been part of her dreams since adolescence, loved her. With her tiger's trust and guidance from Angie's echo, this wonderful man had helped her face the nightmare of her past. They belonged together, were destined for each other.

Zach's cell phone rang at the outskirts of Newport. Jenny laughed. Cell phones were notoriously unreliable along the coastal highway. Whoever it was had probably been trying to reach him for ages.

He whipped into a convenient parking lot and flipped his phone open. "Zach Douglass speaking."

Jenny loved the confident, in-control tone of his voice. Zach knew what he wanted in life. She smiled and thought, *Yes, and he wants me.*

"Calm down, Kate. It can't be that bad."

Biting her lip to keep from speaking, Jenny narrowed her eyes. Kate's timing sucked.

"All right. Relax. Tell James I'm on my way, but I'm not in the city, so it'll be two or three hours." He folded the phone without bothering to say good-bye.

The parking lot shimmered in the noon sun. Zach shut the engine off and turned to face Jenny. "They've uncovered some critical new evidence in the case," he said, a slight frown creasing his forehead. "James flew down from Seattle yesterday. He's waiting for me at his Portland condo. I need to get back to the city."

Jenny leaned close and stroked his cheek. "We have our whole lives ahead of us, Zach. Don't worry about cutting one weekend short."

He caught her fingers to his mouth and kissed them. Her stomach flip-flopped and her nipples peaked, anticipating similar attention. She laughed at herself. *Down, girl! He's yours for the rest of your lives.*

"You're wonderful," he said. "I don't want to go back, but I must." He sighed and checked his watch. "Let's grab a bite here. Then we can head back to the room, check out and start back to the city."

She nodded. "Sounds like a plan. Besides, I'm anxious to see Uncle Andrew." She gave him a vibrant smile. "I have wonderful news to share."

Zach insisted on carrying her lone suitcase all the way to her door and then checked every room of the condo.

"Zach," she said with a laugh, "I've lived here alone for years. I'm perfectly safe. Besides, I thought James needed you on the double."

He growled and pulled her into his arms. "I'm not just dumping you and running. That'd be rude."

She giggled and his cell phone rang again.

"But necessary," she said. "Go. Take care of business and then come back to me." She pushed him out the front door, but lingered to watch him flip open his phone and stride down the hall. When he reached the elevator, he turned and waved, talking all the while.

Jenny stepped inside her apartment and closed the door. She hummed while she unpacked her bag and started a load of laundry. The humming turned to singing when she walked barefoot into the kitchen to study her refrigerator and then her pantry. What to fix Zach for dinner? Something special, something memorable, her first menu in her official capacity as an engaged, soon-to-be-married woman. Yes, special, but not over the top.

She wondered if Zach would mind if she invited Uncle Andrew. Why not? Families celebrated things like engagements, and she and Zach were building a family.

---

Zach reached the condominium tower that housed James' Portland penthouse a few minutes later.

"Good afternoon, Gus," he said to the uniformed doorman. "I'll need the key to the elevator, please."

Gus nodded and handed him a plastic credit card to insert in the elevator's control panel. "Ms. Blackman is already up there," he said. "Have a good evening."

Zach waved the key-card and stepped onto the elevator. "Thanks, Gus. The same to you."

Kate met him at the door. Disheveled hair and a tear-streaked face gave her a wild, hysterical appearance at odds with her neatly pressed black chinos and hunter green blazer. Zach had never seen Kate so agitated. Even when Angie had died, Kate had been a rock.

"Oh, Zach," she cried, throwing herself into his arms. "What took you so long? It's awful and I don't know what to do!"

"Calm down, Kate," Zach said, peeling her arms from around his neck. "Take a deep breath and tell me what's happened."

The distraught woman drew a shuddering breath and ran a trembling hand through her long, dark hair.

"It's James," she said, her voice strained and squeaky. "He's alive, but I can't rouse him."

Zach pushed her out of his way and raced to James' bedroom. "Have you called 9-1-1?"

Kate trailed along behind him, babbling wildly. "His eyes are open ... staring into space.... It's creepy. I don't know what to do. I don't understand. He's ... he's ... not right."

"Kate! Have you called 9-1-1?"

"I, uh, I think so," she said in a shaking voice. "I'm just so rattled. Yes. They'll be here soon."

The door to the bedroom suite stood open and Zach sprinted in. He stopped short when he spotted his employer and friend. Dressed in an impeccably tailored suit of dove gray, James stood frozen on the far side of an impressive hand-carved, four-poster bed. A grotesque statue of himself. His face was contorted, eyes wide, hands balled into fists as though he'd been immobilized in the act of defending himself.

Slowly, Zach crossed the room, taking note of every detail. The love seat leaned precariously against the far wall. A nearby chair sprawled on the floor, legs pointing to the wall. Magazines lay strewn across the deep, plush carpet, and shards of porcelain from a broken lamp littered the floor at James' feet. Zach almost missed the circle of powdered crystal in the mess. Probably moonstone.

Without touching the crystal dust, Zach reached out for James' wrist. Rigid, but warm, the pulse slow and steady. He waved a hand in front of the older man's face. James' eyes flashed, but he didn't move.

Zach considered lowering his shield to contact him psychically, but Angie's echo protested violently, and he didn't have enough information to risk erasing the warding circle. Instead, he turned to face Kate, who cowered near the door.

"How did this happen?" The edge of steel in his voice snapped Kate's hysteria.

"How should I know?"

The sharp reply relieved Zach. He understood Kate, the Arrogant. Kate, the Helpless, frightened him.

"Well," he said, "tell me what you do know."

Kate cast a sideways glance at James and then straightened her shoulders and turned her attention to Zach. "He came down from Seattle yesterday to check on our progress. Said a new informant had contacted the Institute. He seemed particularly interested in Jenny's whereabouts. I tried to find her, but didn't have any luck. He said he'd find her himself. That was last night."

Zach could clear up that mystery, but decided not to interrupt. Kate had finally pulled herself together enough to be sensible.

"We had a lunch appointment to discuss the case. He was going to tell me what he'd learned." She broke off, pressed a trembling hand to her mouth and turned away from Zach while she inhaled several deep breaths. Having regained a measure of control, she continued. "When I arrived, I found him like this."

Suddenly she rounded on Zach, blue eyes blazing, and declared, "She did this! Your precious Jenny! I know she did. He found her last night, confronted her with his new evidence, and ... and ... she did this!"

"What?" Zach couldn't believe his ears. "Kate, are you out of your mind?"

"You don't understand, Zach," she cried, her voice high and strident. "James had proof she killed that man. He came to Portland to confront her. She did this, and because he didn't tell me what his evidence was, she's going to get away with it." The accusation ended in a shrill screech.

"Kate, relax." Zach moved closer to the distraught woman. He took one of her hands in his and patted it gently. "I don't know what happened here, but Jenny wasn't involved."

Kate snorted and gave him a contemptuous glare. "You can't see past your cock. You've been trying to get in her pants since you first laid eyes on her. And Angie not even cold!"

The venom in her voice froze Zach's blood. His heart rate slowed and a cool numbness spread through his limbs. He dropped her hand and stepped away.

"My personal life isn't your concern," he said, his voice icy with anger. "Jenny couldn't have been involved with this." He waved his hand toward James. "She's been with me since Friday afternoon. I took her to the coast this weekend."

"That's not possible!" Kate's eyes bulged and she sputtered. "D-Detective Anderson told her not to leave town. I heard him say it."

Zach's eyes narrowed. He stepped around Kate and strode toward the telephone stationed on James' dresser. "Anderson knows she's not a suspect. He wanted her nearby, as a consultant, nothing more. Besides, I told him we were headed to the coast."

A bizarre sound — a cross between the screech of an angry cat and the whoosh of air from a gut-punched man — made Zach turn. He caught Kate in mid-spring, her nails raking dangerously near his eyes. He scrambled sideways to avoid her claws, but a single fingernail slashed his cheek. Hot blood dribbled across his face. He dabbed at it in amazement.

Kate regained her balance, crouched against the wall a few feet away and touched her bloodied nail to her tongue. A dangerous glint darkened her blue eyes and she dissolved in maniacal laughter.

Pain shredded Zach's mind. His shield collapsed under a sledgehammer assault. The world reeled. A silent, agonized scream exploded into the ether and he slipped toward insensibility. Struggling against the dark, he heard a defiant shriek from Angie's echo.

*No, you can't have him. Not Zach!*

Zach lost his grip on consciousness.

## 23

Uncle Andrew leaned against the doorframe and sipped a glass of Chianti while Jenny tossed a green salad. The lasagna in the oven filled the apartment with the aroma of oregano, garlic and rich, ripe tomatoes.

Andrew grinned when Jenny burst into song. He joined her for the chorus, laughed and said, "I don't think I've ever known you to be this light-hearted and happy. Bless that man for putting such a glow on your face."

She twirled around, picked up the salad bowl and danced with it over to the table. "Yes. I'm deliriously happy. I love Zach, Zach loves me, and we're going to be married." She centered the salad on the creamy white tablecloth, clapped her hands and whirled to face Uncle Andrew. "I'm engaged! Can you believe it? Did you ever dream such a thing would happen to me?"

"Deirdre and Kenneth would be so proud. Their baby has overcome everything life has thrown at her." He set his glass on the counter and crossed the room to give her a hug. "You've taken all those lemons and made an intoxicating margarita." He laughed aloud and ruffled her hair. "Nothing so mundane as lemonade for my girl!"

DEBBIE MUMFORD

A bubble of delight filled her chest and Jenny hugged him back exuberantly. "Thank you, Uncle Andrew. Thank you for being here to celebrate with me." She stepped out of his embrace and led him to the living room. "Dinner is under control. Let's sit down and relax for a few minutes."

She had just settled Uncle Andrew in his favorite easy chair when a scream exploded inside her head. Rubber-legged, she sank onto the couch, breathing in shallow pants.

Zach — in pain!

She labored to orient her thoughts. Somewhere, Zach screamed in agony.

Unbelievable torment ripped through her mind. She fell sideways and curled against the couch's cushions, shrinking into a defensive ball. When the pain-haze lifted and she opened her eyes, Uncle Andrew's worried face hovered inches above her own. He knelt beside her and chafed her trembling hands. Heart hammering, she licked her lips and forced herself to speak.

"It's Zach. Something's happened to Zach." She clutched Uncle Andrew's hands and sat up. "He screamed. The pain ... he's in agony. I felt it, inside my head."

Her head ached, her belly cramped, and her chest tightened. She breathed rapidly and shallowly.

Andrew patted her back, his touch hesitant, uncertain.

"I've got to find him," she cried, "but I don't know how!"

Andrew gripped her shoulders. "Trust your gift, Jenny. Your *second sight* will tell you what you need to know."

Her eyes widened and she stared at him open-mouthed. "Do you really believe that?"

He shook her shoulders gently. "Your gift is genuine, child. I've always known that. I know how hard you've fought it, but it's real. Trust it now."

Jenny threw her arms around his neck. "Thank you," she

whispered. "You can't know what it means to me to hear you say that."

Andrew hugged her close. When he released her, he wiped his eyes and asked, "How can I help?"

"I don't know. I don't know how to start."

"Then try this." He retrieved his wine glass and shoved it into her hand. "Drink some wine and lie back. I'll dim the lights and get you a blanket. Just relax and concentrate on Zach."

Jenny drained the glass and reclined on the couch. Uncle Andrew covered her with a pale blue afghan one of his lady friends had crocheted for her. Warm and as relaxed as she could manage under the circumstances, she approached her tiger. She knelt in front of him and stared into his glowing amber eyes.

*Help me*, she pleaded. *Zach needs us. Help me help him.*

The tiger roared and leapt to his feet.

Jenny's world dissolved into vision.

*A handsome young man lay naked on the floor, limbs splayed. Not dead, merely unconscious.*

*A woman stood across the room. Black hair cascaded across her alabaster back. Softly curling ends brushed naked buttocks. A large, gilt-framed mirror reflected a bowed head, the hands busy with the final preparations for the man's doom. A sheet of loose hair veiled the woman's face.*

*She completed her task and raised her head to stare into the mirror. Kate Blackman glanced at the victim whose heart she intended to rip from his still-living flesh and smiled.*

Cold fear froze Jenny's mind. Zach had gone to Kate.

Jenny struggled to cling to the tiger, to remain in the astral plane. The tiger growled and Jenny wound her arms around his neck and buried her face in coarse fur.

"Show me Zach," she whispered. "No matter where he is or what's happening to him — show me Zach."

The animal's answer rumbled through her chest and her universe shifted.

*Zach lay on the floor, eyes open, but unseeing. Kate knelt beside him, humming tunelessly and unbuckling his belt.*

Jenny's stomach revolted. A wave of bile surged into her throat. The bitter, acid taste burned her tongue.

Kate intended to sacrifice Zach.

---

Jenny's eyes flew open and she stared wildly around the room. Uncle Andrew paced around the living room like a caged animal, his restlessness and irritation a tangible presence. She pushed herself upright and he sprinted to her side, grabbed her wrist and checked her pulse.

"Are you all right? Did you find Zach?" His voice quavered and his desire to help pulsed through her too sensitive mind.

"Kate," she whispered, locking her gaze to her uncle's. "It's been Kate all along. She used the rune book, killed to gain psychic power, and now she's got Zach." Jenny's voice rose, shrill and hysterical. "She's going to kill Zach!"

Uncle Andrew reached for her, but she sprang from the couch and sprinted to the entry closet. She ripped open the door and grabbed a jacket. Her hand gripped the front doorknob when Uncle Andrew caught her shoulder and spun her around to face him.

"Where do you think you're going, Jennifer Elaine?" His voice was tight with strain and his face mirrored her fear. "Call the police. Tell them where she is, what she's done. Let them handle it."

She wrenched away from him, but paused at the door. "You don't understand. They can't stop her." She closed her eyes and leaned her head against the smooth wooden frame. "I've got to go!"

She whirled back to Andrew and threw her arms around his neck. "I love you, Uncle," she whispered. "You've been my anchor in this life, but Zach is my universe. I can't sit on the couch while Kate destroys him."

"At least tell me where you're going," he pleaded, "so *I* can call the police. Detective Anderson will back you up."

Jenny laughed, a grating, humorless sound. She gave Andrew one last squeeze, released him and opened the door.

"Detective Anderson thinks I'm unbalanced and unreliable, but go ahead and call him. Send him to James Towne's penthouse. I don't know the address, but it's downtown."

She raced for the elevator without a backward glance, wondering if she'd ever see her uncle again.

## 24

————

Jenny wove through traffic, terror congealing her blood each time a red light forced her to stop. She tried to calm herself with deep breathing techniques, but couldn't focus on anything but Zach. The thought of him lying unconscious in Kate's hands twisted Jenny's guts and drenched her scalp in cold sweat.

The location of James' penthouse mystified her conscious mind, but the tiger guided her with skill and confidence. *Left at the light; straight across the bridge; continue past the MAX station; there — Zach's in the rose stone building with the awning.*

When she arrived at the posh condominium complex, she sensed her quarry prowling on the top floor. Her tires screeched and she peeled into the visitor parking lot. She slammed out of her car and raced toward the elevator that would carry her to the guarded main door.

She caught her breath on the interminably slow ride. It wouldn't do to alarm the doorman. Forcing herself to breathe slowly and maintain a calm demeanor, she stepped into the parking structure's small entrance lobby and faced a uniformed guard.

"May I have your name, Miss?" The man's tone brooked no disobedience.

Jenny glanced past him at the crystal clear, securely locked, glass doors and sighed. Of course, James Towne lived in a secure building.

"Jennifer Murdoch," she said. "I'm here to see James Towne. It's urgent."

The man consulted a list, nodded and pushed an unseen button. The doors buzzed and swung inward.

"When you reach the elevator, use this card." He handed her a plastic key card. "It will allow you to reach the penthouse."

"Thank you," Jenny said, barely managing to suppress a sob. She snatched the card from his extended hand and hurried through the open doors to the elevators on the far side of the beautifully appointed lobby.

Jenny paced the elevator's small enclosure and chewed her lower lip. Her gaze darted to the lighted numbers above the door each time the soft chime announced a floor's passage. When she reached the penthouse, Kate would be waiting. Surprise was Jenny's sole advantage. Kate had to remain unaware of her approach.

Jenny didn't have a clue how to use her gift aggressively, but she'd find a way. The tiger gave her information, sometimes more than she knew how to handle, but he'd had precious little experience guiding her psychokinetic ability. She couldn't work magic, couldn't weave spells to disorient or disable. She had no clear idea how to stop Kate and save Zach, but she had to try.

And she knew, without a doubt, she stood a better chance of succeeding than Detective Anderson and his non-gifted officers.

The elevator doors whooshed quietly open — directly into James' living room. No hallway or foyer offered her a final opportunity to collect her thoughts. Fortifying her strongest psychic barrier, she stepped from the elevator car directly into Kate's stronghold.

Heart pounding, palms sweating, afraid to breathe lest she alert her enemy, Jenny tiptoed across the living room. Thick green carpet muffled her steps, but fear clogged her throat and threatened to choke her. A few more steps and she could lean against the wall, support herself with something other than rubbery legs.

The tiger hunkered down, tense, ready to spring into action. He assured her of Zach's presence — Zach's *living* presence — in the next room.

James' bedroom. She reached the door, flattened herself against the wall to one side of the frame, took a moment to gulp air and steady herself. Hands splayed against the wall, she inched toward the opening and peered around the doorjamb.

Zach lay naked on the plush green carpet, arms and legs spread-eagled and aligned to form four points of a pentacle. His head made the fifth point. A shining band of pulverized moonstone surrounded his body in a perfect circle. Stripes of the shimmering substance crossed his ankles, wrists and throat. The sacrificial victim, immobile ... and awake!

Zach couldn't turn his head, but Jenny detected eye-movement. His gaze skittered wildly around the room searching, she surmised, for any sign of hope.

Jenny forced her attention from her beloved. Time to assess the situation logically. Kate wasn't in sight, but the bathroom door stood open and water splashed full-force into the tub.

She almost cried out when she caught sight of James. He stood in a corner across from the bed, frozen in an unnatural position. Like Zach, he was immobile, but conscious. His eyes flashed with anger ... and fear. Kate had positioned James so he had no choice but to watch the preparations for Zach's final act of paranormal research.

James possessed a powerful psychic talent. Kate's ability to hold him immobile terrified Jenny.

The tiger rumbled and twitched his tail, but remained in a stealthy crouch. Jenny had followed him into the event stream to find Zach. Now she followed his golden-eyed gaze toward James. She nodded and sent a cautious tendril of thought curling into the older psychic's consciousness, a delicate probe designed to dissipate if Kate maintained an active link to James' mind.

James answered the whisper-soft touch and clung to Jenny's perception. *She's not in the bedroom, Jenny. She disabled my body and my ability to initiate contact and then withdrew.*

Jenny strengthened the contact and sought to reassure him. *I'm right outside the door. I'll get you out of here. Do you know what she intends to do?*

*Oh, yes.* His thoughts dripped outrage. *Zach's her first victim tonight, but I'll be next. She had Zach so focused on me, he didn't stand a chance.*

*I won't leave,* Jenny sent. *No one's going to die. I won't let her finish the ritual. Not this time.*

She maintained a light touch in James' mind and sent a careful tendril toward Zach. She expected to be deflected by his shields, but entered his mind with the equivalent of a psychic shout. His shields no longer existed.

Zach winced. At least, his eyes did.

*Jenny?* He pushed the silent question back along her probe. *I'm hallucinating. Jenny can't be here. Is that you, Angie?*

*You were right the first time. It's Jenny. I'm here, Zach. I'm in your mind and in the apartment.*

A wave of fear engulfed him and Jenny struggled to stay above it. Faced with horrible mutilation and death, her safety remained his first concern.

She sent an answering wave of calm and repose.

Her next communication flowed along both tendrils,

updating both men on the situation. *I'm alone, but help is on the way. I don't have to defeat Kate, just delay her. Uncle Andrew is sending Detective Anderson.*

Her last contact touched Zach alone, an intimate caress. *I love you. I won't let her hurt you.*

Jenny withdrew both tendrils and closed her mind behind the strongest shield her tiger could provide. Taking several deep, cleansing breaths, she wiped her sweaty palms on her jeans, whirled around the doorframe into James' bedroom and raced for the bathroom door. Before Kate could react, Jenny slammed the door shut.

The door locked on Kate's side, but the tiger showed Jenny the lock assembly. She ignored her hammering heart and concentrated on moving the small mechanical elements. Sweat beaded her forehead.

Kate's soft footfalls sounded on the other side. The door-knob turned in Jenny's sweat-slickened hand.

The tiger roared and the lock clicked into place, but the task wasn't complete. Kate could open the lock with a twist of her hand. Jenny had to change the metal's physical state and fuse the bolt in place.

"Is that you, Jenny?" Kate's voice drifted through the door, silky and sweet. "Do you really think you can hold this door against me? Go home, little girl. You're not up to this."

Jenny refused to take the bait. Instead, she focused every shred of her newfound ability on holding the bolt stationary while the tiger chuffed and growled. The doorknob remained still in her hand.

*Come on, Tiger,* she pleaded silently. *Help me!*

The handle gave an infinitesimal turn. The bolt slid back the tiniest fraction. Jenny's heart leapt to her throat when the knob shook violently in her hand.

"You know I'm stronger than you," Kate taunted. "You don't

trust your talent. You don't want your talent. You're no match for me."

"Shut up!" Jenny cried, a flare of anger surging through her. The tiger pounced, directed the emotional energy into the mechanism, slammed the bolt home and fused it in place.

Jenny released the knob and slid to the floor, unsure whether sweat or tears blurred her vision. The locked door wouldn't hold Kate for long, but the small victory buoyed Jenny's confidence.

She pushed herself upright, dashed to Zach and smudged the crystal circle with her foot. The dust scattered and swirled as the bound power inside the pentacle released. Kneeling over her lover, she blew the moonstone stripes from Zach's neck and wrists, careful not to touch the powder lest she ignite its latent energy and strengthen his bonds.

She kissed him quickly and sprinted to James. "Release your legs," she called over her shoulder, "but don't touch the moonstone dust with bare skin. I'll try to release James."

Before she reached James, the bathroom door shattered and she whirled to find Kate striding toward Zach, whose crystal-dusted ankles still bound him to the floor.

"Kate," Jenny shouted, fortifying her voice with a psychic stab. "Leave him alone!"

The enraged woman turned mid-stride and stopped. Her long, dark hair settled behind her shoulders, revealing a statuesque body sheathed in a see-through red negligee. Her feet were bare and she had removed her jewelry. Eyes snapping fire, she focused on Jenny.

"Well, now," she said, clenching her fists. "You're becoming a nuisance, my dear." She smiled, an expression devoid of humor. "What do you think of your boyfriend now? Naked ... in a bedroom with me." She licked her lips and stepped closer to

Zach. "He's a good lover, but then, you already knew that, didn't you?"

Kate probed Jenny's defenses. The tiger roared. Jenny stood her ground. No doubt, Kate hoped to goad her into releasing control of her shields.

"Zach's an excellent lover," Jenny agreed, "but you'll just have to take my word for it. He wouldn't soil himself with someone like you."

Kate scowled and glanced briefly at Zach. Jenny seized her opportunity and lowered her shields long enough to hurl a bolt of psychic energy into Kate's body. The woman's stricken expression testified to the accuracy of the blow. Kate stumbled back a pace. Jenny sprinted across the room and placed herself between Kate and the men.

When the spasm passed, Kate snarled and launched herself at Jenny, nails slashing like talons.

The force of Kate's attack knocked Jenny off-balance and she tumbled onto the bed. Kate raked her long nails at Jenny's face, but Jenny grabbed her hand and held it off. Jenny's arms quivered and she didn't know how long she could hold the other woman away. Kate had the advantage of weight and momentum.

Jenny glanced wildly around the room, caught sight of a pair of scissors in a pencil holder on the bedside table. The scissors levitated, flew across the room and embedded themselves in Kate's back. Kate howled with pain, released Jenny and rolled off the bed, twisting to pull the sharp instrument from her back.

Out of the corner of her eye, Jenny noticed Zach reach toward his ankles. "Zach," she cried, scrambling from the bed and sprinting out of Kate's reach. "Don't touch the powdered moonstone! Blow it off."

"No!" Kate screamed. She turned the scissors in her hand and lunged toward Zach. "This is my legacy, my birthright! I'm not finished with you yet!"

"Oh yes, you are," Jenny said through gritted teeth. Summoning all her strength, she focused her tiger on the black-haired witch, lowered her shields and sent a white-hot bolt of energy crashing into Kate's mind. The woman's defenses crumbled. Her mind lay bare, open to Jenny's power.

The warped, slimy mess of Kate's thoughts repelled Jenny, but a vision of the rune book caught and held her attention. Jenny followed the elusive thought to a cottage in Ireland.

*Firelight dancing on mud-daubed walls... bubbling cauldron steaming fetid fumes into the closed room ... decaying, white-eyed human heads hanging from rafters ... the rune book open, a blood dipped quill abandoned across one corner ... a man screaming, splayed on the floor, his voice raw, and incoherent ... blood pouring from between his legs ... a filthy, matted-haired version of Kate ripping his chest open with a dagger...*

Jenny shuddered and pulled away from the witch's mind. Her withdrawal afforded Kate the opportunity to cast a rudimentary barrier. She repelled Jenny from her psyche entirely and ran screaming at her, scissors raised menacingly.

Terror exploded through Jenny's mind and body. The taller woman bore down on her, weapon gleaming. Jenny froze — a deer in the headlights of an oncoming truck. At the last moment, her brain snapped into gear and she dropped to the floor, rolled sideways and kicked Kate's ankle, tripping her neatly.

Kate's body hit the floor with a resounding smack and the scissors flew from her fist. Jenny scrambled after the scissors, turned to deflect Kate's next attack ... and sank to the floor in relief.

Zach had launched himself at his erstwhile assistant and had pinned her to the floor.

"You wanted me to mount you," he said, face grim. "Well, this is as close as you're ever going to get."

A completely nude Zach straddled Kate's barely clad frame. He slammed her wrists against the floor above her head and fought to hold her lower body immobile with his legs. His rage-engorged shaft hovered dangerously near her pubis and she stilled, recognizing the suggestiveness of their position.

"Go ahead," Kate taunted. "You know you want me." Her eyes glowed with triumph and she bucked her hips, bringing her curly-haired triangle enticingly near his manhood.

Zach shifted away from her, but without releasing his hold on her body. "I wouldn't risk the contamination. You disgust me." He looked away from her, clearly seeking Jenny.

Their eyes met and, disheveled and angry though she was, Jenny relaxed. Jealousy wasn't an issue.

Fierce pride surged through Jenny. She ached in muscles she hadn't known she possessed and her breath came in ragged gasps, but she grinned at Zach, punched her fist in the air and gave a whoop of victory. Zach's face lit with triumph.

Kate screamed, rage and despair equally evident in the strident sound.

"Sweetheart," Zach said over the din of the witch's howls, "can you shut her up — maybe immobilize her? Like she did James? I can't stand touching her."

"Hold on," Jenny said, her heart bursting with a curious mixture of anger, pride and love. "I want back-up before I lower my shields again."

Jenny turned and sprinted to James' side. She blurred the small crystal circle that had kept her from freeing James and touched both men's minds, releasing their psychic abilities.

"Thank you, Jenny," James said. "For everything." He breathed a sigh of relief, rubbed his cramped muscles and grinned at Zach. "It'll be a relief to get you dressed again, man. I've seen way too much of you today."

Zach scowled at his friend. "I liked you better mute," he retorted.

Through their unaccustomed three-way link, Jenny and James heard Angie's ghost whisper to Zach, *"Shields up!"*

A second later, Kate bucked beneath Zach and aimed a final pulse of scorching energy at their linked consciousness. Jenny's tiger reacted with brutal swiftness. The force of Jenny/tiger's rage pushed the deranged woman over the edge and into unconsciousness.

"Damn, Jenny," whispered James. "Your tiger has amazing reflexes!"

The whoosh of the elevator doors, followed by a thud of booted feet startled the three friends. Zach jumped away from Kate's slack body, grabbed his clothes from a nearby chair and dashed for the privacy of the bathroom.

James strode from the bedroom, smoothing his hair and adjusting his mussed clothing, to meet Detective Anderson and fill him in on the incident.

Jenny dropped onto the end of the bed and gazed at her defeated adversary. She wouldn't completely relax until Anderson had the murdering witch in handcuffs.

No, that wasn't true. She wouldn't be comfortable until Kate was incarcerated in a mental institution with her cell warded against psychic energy. She hoped James had the political pull to ensure the proper safety precautions were put in place.

She studied the fallen woman's body until the bed sagged beside her. Without looking up, she reached over and put her hand on Zach's jeans-encased knee. She smiled. Zach was safe, whole and fully clothed. He had survived ... and so had she.

## 25

By the time Detective Anderson satisfied himself that all three accounts of the day's events coincided, Jenny, Zach and James were exhausted. Soon after Anderson and his men arrived, Jenny telephoned Uncle Andrew and reassured the elderly man of everyone's safety. James took the phone away from her and thanked Andrew profusely for his part in the rescue.

Detective Anderson, though anxious to question Kate, agreed to James' suggestion to keep the woman sedated during transport to the lock-down ward at the hospital.

"I understand your reluctance to believe all this, Detective," James said, "but trust me, until she's incarcerated in a facility capable of dealing with her ... special abilities, Kate is a menace. For the safety of the men who'll be transporting her, keep her sedated."

Anderson started to argue, but Jenny stopped him. "Detective Anderson," she said quietly. "Take a look at these two men. They've admitted to being held captive by this attractive woman. Do you think they're proud to let you know she got the better of them? She intended to slice them up like that other poor guy."

She shook her head and frowned at Anderson. "James and Zach are both extremely intelligent and in peak physical condition. If Kate managed to get them in a position where their lives were in jeopardy, well, better safe than sorry, don't you think?"

Anderson scowled at each of them in turn, but finally agreed. "Fine. Mr. Towne, work it out with the EMT and his supervising physician. I'll question her later at the hospital." He shrugged and nodded to Jenny. "It's no more than the inconvenience you went through at her suggestion."

Jenny's heart leapt to her throat. "What do you mean?"

"I mean," he said with a wry grin, "Kate informed us she'd seen you performing occult rituals. She was the reason I had you in lock-down a couple of weeks back."

Zach put his arm around Jenny and gave her a reassuring hug. "I wondered why you were so hell-bent on locking Jenny up." Zach and the detective stared at each other. "I can assure you, this time you have the right woman in custody."

Anderson nodded. "I don't pretend to understand or believe half of what you people are telling me went on here today, but there's sufficient physical evidence to link this crime to the murder scene. I don't think the DA will have any trouble deciding to prosecute." He surveyed the room, which swarmed with criminal investigators gathering evidence. "What I don't know is whether a judge will find her competent to stand trial."

James shrugged. "As long as she's kept out of normal society, I don't guess it matters whether she's in prison or a mental hospital." He glanced at the remains of the pentagram on the floor and looked at Zach. "I'm going to make sure I'm notified before anyone even thinks of releasing her, though." He shuddered. "I don't ever want to go through anything like this again."

"Amen," said Jenny.

Anderson grimaced and escaped across the room to answer a question for one of his men.

Jenny turned to James. "Speaking of not going through this again, what are you going to do about the rune book? That's the real culprit"

"I know. When I can get it back from the authorities, I'm going to destroy it." He arched an eyebrow at her. "I'll need several strong psychics to do it. Would you consider helping?"

She nodded, warm relief flooding her system. "Nothing would give me greater pleasure." She shivered and Zach tightened his embrace. "You did warn them to quarantine that volume didn't you?"

"I did," James said, leading them into a spacious study, away from the activity of the crime scene investigators. "Angie died to protect Zach from its evil. I wouldn't be honoring her sacrifice if I allowed it to take hold of another human mind."

Silence reigned for a moment while Zach and James remembered their golden-haired friend. James ran a hand through his hair and dropped into a well-worn leather chair facing a large window with a panoramic view of the Willamette River. Zach folded his lanky frame onto the matching couch and pulled Jenny down beside him. She relaxed against the comfortable surface and closed her eyes. Exhaustion weighed against her concentration.

"By the way," said Zach. "Do we know how Kate fell under the book's influence? She wasn't always like this, you know."

"I know," Jenny said, forcing her eyes open. "I found the answer when I touched her mind. The rune book belonged to Kate's ancestral family. It had been warded, safe from intruders, unless and until a woman of the original witch's bloodline touched it. Kate had heard stories about it and she visited Ireland with the intention of finding the book. When she did, the temptation was too much for her.

"Once she got her hands on it, she discovered she understood it without translation. Her blood called the legacy to life.

The runes spoke to her, whispered dark promises, and she believed. She developed a symbiotic relationship with the book. The runes taught Kate, and she sacrificed to feed the runes — and her power grew."

"Unbelievable," Zach said, shaking his head. "Too bad someone in her family didn't destroy it long ago."

"They probably didn't know how," said James. "I tested Kate when she came to work for the Institute. She didn't have more than trace levels of psychic ability. If no one else in her ancestral line exhibited the gift, they were better off leaving the book under its protective wards."

"The real shame is that Kate found it. If she hadn't come in contact with those runes, Angie would still be alive."

"Speaking of Angie," Jenny said when the silence became protracted, "I'd swear I heard her speak to us just before Kate's final attack." She glanced between the men, her mouth suddenly dry. "Did either of you hear her?"

"Yes," whispered James.

"Definitely," said Zach, tracing a line of stitching on the arm of the couch, "but, now that you mention it, I haven't heard anything from her since Kate went down." He frowned and an odd expression crossed his features. "I think she's gone."

"Maybe she only stayed to finish what she started," Jenny said quietly. Both men looked quizzical, so she continued. "She died protecting Zach from Kate and the book. Maybe she couldn't — or wouldn't — leave until the danger had been averted. With Kate in custody, she's fulfilled her task."

"I hope she's at peace," said Zach, turning to stare into Jenny's eyes. "She was right on both counts: the rune book was dangerous, and you're perfect for me." He tore his gaze from Jenny and smiled at James. "I haven't had a chance to tell you. Jenny's agreed to marry me."

"Congratulations," said James. He clapped his hands

together and smiled broadly. "I hope the rest of your lives together will be peaceful, not like tonight."

"Absolutely," Jenny agreed, "but before we drop the topic, I have a question. Why was I able to reach Zach when I arrived? Why in the world did you dismantle your shield tonight of all times?"

"I didn't. I don't know what happened," Zach told her. "My shield was in place, and then Kate breached it. No idea how she managed it."

"I can explain that," said James. "I observed the whole thing, though I couldn't move. Your blood gave her the advantage she needed. Remember? Kate scratched your face and then licked your blood from her finger. Until that moment, she hadn't been able to affect you. Ingesting your blood allowed her to pass your shields."

Zach's face paled.

"Of course," said Jenny. "The blood gave her a physical connection to you." She scooted closer to Zach and pressed her face against his shoulder to hide the tears welling in her eyes. "I'm so lucky you're alive," she whispered. "I don't think I could have survived if she'd killed you."

Zach rested his cheek against Jenny's hair and held her close.

James coughed quietly, slapped his hands against his knees and stood. "I think Detective Anderson needs me," he said and left the two lovers alone.

"I'm a lucky man," Zach said after a moment, "to be loved by such an amazing woman." He slid a finger under Jenny's chin and raised her head to face him. His eyes shone with pride. "You fought like a tiger in there. I'd never have believed the quiet, self-contained young woman I first met would've had such a warrior spirit."

She smiled up at him, ignoring the trickle of tears running down her cheeks. "It's amazing what you're capable of when you accept the tiger in your soul. Besides, you promised to marry me. No way was I letting you slip away."

Zach grinned broadly and lowered his head to capture her lips in a soul-scorching kiss.

The tiger roared his approval, and Jenny's fears and anxiety dissolved in the safety of Zach's embrace.

# ALSO BY DEBBIE MUMFORD

### Kristi Lundrigan Mysteries:

- Delectable Mountain Quilting (Novel)
- Fool's Puzzle (Short Story)
- Wildfire! (Short Story)

### Gus and Ghost Short Story Series:

- Seventh
- Seventh: First Fruits
- Death of an Alchemist (Uncollected Anthology)
- Seventh: The Samhain Dilemma

### Logans of Lastalrig Series:

- Her Highland Laird (Novella)
- Her Highland Yule (Short Story)

### Red's Series:

- Red's Magick (Short Story Collection)
- Seeing Red (Short Story)

### Signs of the Prophecy Novels:

- Youngest
- Seeker
- Chosen (Coming Soon!)

**Sorcha's Children Series:**

- SORCHA'S CHILDREN (OMNIBUS EDITION)
- SORCHA'S HEART (NOVELLA)
- DRAGONS' CHOICE (NOVEL)
- DRAGONS' FLIGHT (NOVEL)
- DRAGONS' DESIRE (NOVEL)
- DRAGONS' DESTINY (NOVEL)

**Supernatural Yellowstone Short Story Series:**

- REALITY BITES
- THE CAT LADY OF YELLOWSTONE

**Universal Star League Short Story Series:**

- THE WARBIRDS OF ABSAROKA
- AWAKENING THE WARRIOR
- INCIDENT ON THE ODYSSEY
- THE QUEEN'S CAPTIVE
- THE LOST COLONY
- VOYAGES INTO THE BLACK (COLLECTION)

**Witchling Short Story Series:**

- WITCHLING
- THE SOLITARY SORCERESS
- TO PROTECT A PRINCESS

**Stand Alone Novels:**

- SECOND SIGHT

**Short Story Collections:**

- Love in a Flash
- Tales of Bygone Days
- Tales of Love & Magick
- Tales of the Unexpected
- Tales of Tomorrow
- Tales of Disastrous Deeds

**Short Fiction:**

- A Walk with Georgia
- Adrenaline Junkie
- Astromancer
- Beneath and Beyond
- Deep Dreaming
- Delia's Decision
- Ice Storm
- Incident on the High Line
- Miss Bainbridge's Summer Adventure
- Needle-Green
- New Year
- Opening Her Eyes
- Remembrance
- Silver-Tipped Death
- Sisters in Suffrage
- Skye Dreams
- Spinning
- The Tie That Binds
- The Trail Where We Cried
- The White Dragon and the Red
- To Dream of Flying
- Treasures

- WAKINYAN'S VALLEY

**"WDM Presents" Anthologies:**

- 2016: A YEAR OF SHORT FICTION
- 2017: A YEAR OF SHORT FICTION
- TALES OF MYSTERY & MAYHEM

## DELECTABLE MOUNTAIN QUILTING PREVIEW

If you enjoyed *Second Sight*, you may want to read *Delectable Mountain Quilting*, a quilt themed cozy mystery. Here's a sample chapter.

Kristiana Lundrigan, Kristi to her friends and family, stared out the picture window beside her breakfast table. She adored the view, showing as it did the majestic Absaroka Range, including Mount Cowen, the highest peak visible from her Paradise Valley home. Scooping the last bite of scrambled eggs onto her fork, she concentrated on allowing the peace of the mountain scenery to soothe her soul. Today would be exciting, perhaps even nerve-wracking. She wanted to start it as calmly as possible.

Her small house sat on the eastern edge of Garnet Gateway, Montana, giving her an unimpeded view of the open valley as it approached the foothills of the 'Sorkees. Kristi had known it was the home she'd been searching for the moment she saw it. Single story, three bedrooms, and a nicely updated bathroom with an old fashioned claw footed tub. The view from the breakfast nook had been the cherry on top as far as Kristi was concerned.

She'd converted the east facing bedroom into a quilting studio, leaving the other two for a guest bedroom and her own use.

Designing her studio had been a delight. She'd finally had the space to create a floor-to-ceiling design wall by installing sheets of flannel-covered Homasote board on the largest unbroken wall. The flannel was the perfect touch. No need to pin her blocks to the wall (though the Homasote board was porous enough to allow for that if needed), they adhered to the flannel effortlessly.

Her sewing table, with its state-of-the-art Viking machine, sat in front of the room's only window, with the large cutting table on her left and the design wall to her right. Her ironing station stood behind her, near the closet, which had had its sliding doors removed and shelves built in to hold Kristi's fabric stash, stored quilts, and as-yet-unfinished projects. The final touch had been turning one of her early quilts into a Roman shade and hanging it over the entrance to the closet, protecting her stash of brightly colored fabric from too much light.

Kristi picked up her mug of mint tea from the scrubbed oak breakfast table and sipped the fragrant brew.

The divorce had been a painful blow, but it was in her past now. She was her own woman at last, with a home that suited her, and— in less than a week!— a business of her own. She was no longer Jason's wife, nor was she her father's little girl. She was Kristiana Lundrigan, quilter, teacher, and soon-to-be business woman. An upstanding member of the Garnet Gateway community.

Garnet Gateway. She loved this small Montana town, nestled serenely in the Paradise Valley and guarded by the imposing Absaroka Mountains. She wasn't a native, hadn't been born in the town or even on one of the surrounding ranches, but Garnet Gateway was her home. Had been since she followed Jason here after her graduation from Montana State University in Bozeman. She'd been ready to follow him to Denver, where he'd worked his way up from patrol officer to homicide detective, but Jason had chosen to return home to Montana, to Garnet Gateway.

She'd married in Garnet Gateway. Established her first real home here, and had planned to grow old and die here. Still did, as a matter of fact. Only now she was alone.

Well, maybe not *exactly* alone.

As if summoned by her thought, Stitches and Between, her moggy cats, strolled into the kitchen and hopped lightly onto the window seat beside the table to join her. Stitches, the older of the pair, was a gray tabby female with four white paws. Between, named for the tiny, sharp needles used in hand quilting, was a little tuxedo male with the personality of a perennial kitten. Though Stitches was hardly a big cat, she outweighed Between by a good two pounds. The pair were best friends and excellent companions for Kristi.

"Well, good morning, you two," Kristi said, taking a moment to scratch behind first Stitches' ears and then Between's. "What have you been up to while I was eating?"

Stitches settled onto the cushioned window seat, front paws

folded beneath her chest, purring contentedly, while Between nipped Kristi's finger gently... always ready to remind her that she was *his* human. He was happy to share her affection with Stitches, of course, but Between was a possessive little fellow.

Kristi nodded. "I love you too, Between." She understood possessive. And loyalty. And trust.

Jason, her ex-husband, had failed in all three areas. He'd had a brief affair during an out of town convention, and while he'd been honest enough to confess (when she confronted him with clear evidence), he'd failed to understand her possessiveness, or her expectation of loyalty, or that he'd forfeited her trust. He'd expected her to forgive and forget and for their lives to continue as if his indiscretion had never happened.

Unfortunately for him, Kristi wasn't built that way. She was too aware of her own worth to allow herself to be treated with such casual disrespect.

None of that changed the fact that she loved him.

Always had.

Always would.

But she'd divorced him anyway.

She refused to live with a man she couldn't trust, so despite a broken heart, she did what needed to be done and moved forward into a new, solitary life.

But when she closed her eyes...

...it was Jason's face that floated to the top of her consciousness.

He might not fit every woman's definition of handsome, but he had always been her gold standard. High forehead, strong jaw, steely gray eyes that could go all soft and almost blue when his emotions were high.

She tried to keep him out of her thoughts, and was mostly successful during the day... but nights were a different matter.

When she climbed into bed each night, usually with a cat

curled on either side, she'd dream of Jason. Of running her fingers through his wavy chestnut hair, the thick mass of it like silk between her fingers. Or she'd giggle again as his unshaven chin scratched her cheek after a sensuous night of intimate pleasure.

And... Oh!... did she dream of the pleasures of making love to him!

Only to wake at dawn mourning the loss of the life they'd built together. The life she'd expected to continue until death parted them.

Busyness kept her going. She exorcised Jason from her days by constant activity. Meetings with the divorce attorney. Moving from the home they had shared into an apartment until their affairs (what an appropriate word!) were settled. Designing quilt patterns and then choosing fabrics and making sample blocks. Anything to keep herself from remembering that he had betrayed her. That he didn't love her... or at least didn't love her enough.

When the dust settled and the divorce was final, Kristi found that she had sufficient funds to buy a house in Garnet Gateway. She launched herself into the real estate market, determined to find the perfect home. She knew exactly what she wanted: a small house with enough space for a dedicated quilting studio; and when she found it, she didn't hesitate.

Not quite a year as a single woman and Kristi had taken back her maiden name, bought a home, and adopted Stitches and Between. She'd just begun to think about quitting her part-time secretarial job and establishing a career as a quilt artist when she'd learned that the local quilt shop was for sale.

Talk about perfect timing!

She'd made an appointment with her accountant, crunched some pretty amazing numbers, and determined that the inheritance her maternal grandmother had left her would be enough to not only make the down payment, but would allow for some remodeling if she planned carefully.

Nanna Van Oss would be pleased and proud to know she'd helped Kristi realize her dream of owning her own business, and a quilt shop was an apt use for the money. After all, Nanna was the one who'd taught Kristi to quilt.

Kristi had toured the quilt shop that very day, jotting down ideas for how she would use the space, as well as noting renovations that she'd want to see made. She'd made an offer that same afternoon, and then, praying for a quick acceptance, had begun to load her stitches, nice and even, so that when she pulled the needle through she wouldn't have to stop and pick any of them out.

She'd filled out the application for a small business loan, set up telephone interviews with several contractors, and used her notes to draw up plans for the renovations she hoped to make. With her plans in place, she'd settled back to wait for the current owner's response.

Mattie Stebbings, while not exactly a friend, was someone she knew on sight. Kristi often bought her quilting cottons from Mattie's shop and the women were both members of the statewide quilt guild. Kristi had hoped that Mattie would find her an acceptable beneficiary for the shop.

The wait hadn't been long. Less than twenty-four hours after the offer was made, Mattie accepted. Kristi's small business loan was also approved in short order, and the closing for the quilt shop was fast-tracked. In a mere thirty days, Kristi would own *Delectable Mountain Quilting*!

That was twenty-five days ago. Closing was now only five days away. Come Monday, the shop would be hers.

Time to meet with her chosen contractor and set the wheels in motion.

That was her agenda for today.

She'd arranged to meet Mark Robards, her contractor, at the shop this morning. Mattie, who seemed unusually anxious to consummate the sale, had closed the store as soon as she'd accepted Kristi's offer for the business, which included the building, land, and inventory, so the realtor, Stacy Akins, would also be present. Kristi intended to outline her desired changes and expected Mark to provide a detailed estimate of the cost.

Turning her gaze to the mountains once more, Kristi took a deep breath, held it for a moment, then released it slowly. Everything was going to work out. She just knew it. Mark would give her a reasonable bid; the remainder of Nanna Van Oss's gift would more than cover the work; and the closing papers would be signed on Monday.

Each stitch in the last twenty-five days had followed the last, neat as a pin. These final steps would as well.

Glancing at the cats, she grinned. "It's going to be an exciting day, kids. You two will soon be quilt store cats!"

---

Look for *Delectable Mountain Quilting* at your favorite online retailer.

# ABOUT DEBBIE MUMFORD

Debbie Mumford specializes in speculative fiction—fantasy, paranormal romance, and science fiction. Author of the popular *Sorcha's Children* series, Debbie loves the unknown, whether it's the lure of space or earthbound mythology. Her work has been published in multiple volumes of *Fiction River*, as well as in *Heart's Kiss Magazine*, *Spinetingler Magazine*, and other popular markets. She writes about dragon-shifters, time-traveling lovers, and ghostly detectives for adults as Debbie Mumford and contemporary fantasy for tweens and young adults as Deb Logan.

Join Debbie's special announcement newsletter list and receive a FREE story!

*To learn more, visit Debbie at:*
debbiemumford.com/
*Or send her an email at:*
deborah.mumford@gmail.com

facebook.com/DebbieMumfordWrites
amazon.com/author/debbiemumford
bookbub.com/authors/debbie-mumford
twitter.com/deborah_mumford